"We're standing under the mistletoe."

"Christian."

"Come on," he urged. "It's tradition."

Apprehension coursed through her. She didn't like being the center of attention, but she longed to feel Christian's lips against hers again. No one would say anything if it was just a mistletoe kiss.

As she parted her lips, he lowered his mouth to capture hers.

Sparks. Again. She nearly gasped at the intensity of them. Nothing could compare to Christian's kisses. His lips pressed against hers with desire and longing. Matching the pressure, she leaned into him, eager to get closer.

She wanted more of his kiss, more of him.

Dear Reader,

Once again, I find myself in Hood Hamlet, Oregon. I wanted everyone in the quaint mountain town to experience a little Christmas magic this time, but most especially Leanne Thomas!

Leanne made brief appearances in *Rescued by the Magic of Christmas* and *Christmas Magic on the Mountain*. She also appeared in *Snow-Kissed Reunion*, my Harlequin.com online read. Each time I wrote about her, I thought she would make a great romance heroine.

Leanne Thomas is a mountain rescue volunteer with Oregon Mountain Search and Rescue (OMSAR) and a paramedic with Hood Hamlet Fire & Rescue. Whether at work or play, she's surrounded by men. She tries hard to be "one of the guys." I wondered what kind of man it would take to break through Leanne's tough exterior and melt her heart.

As I researched women firefighters, I learned quite a few marry other firefighters. I thought a firefighter might be a good match for Leanne. Enter Christian Welton, the handsome, young rookie at the fire station, who is also a rock climber.

Neither asked for "love" when writing their Christmas lists, but sometimes what we want isn't what we need. And no matter what's happened in the past, it's never too late to believe in Christmas magic and happy endings.

Enjoy!

Melissa

MELISSA McCLONE
Firefighter Under the Mistletoe

TORONTO NEW YORK LONDON
AMSTERDAM PARIS SYDNEY HAMBURG
STOCKHOLM ATHENS TOKYO MILAN MADRID
PRAGUE WARSAW BUDAPEST AUCKLAND

Recycling programs
for this product may
not exist in your area.

ISBN-13: 978-0-373-17765-3

FIREFIGHTER UNDER THE MISTLETOE

First North American Publication 2011

Copyright © 2011 by Melissa Martinez McClone

www.Harlequin.com

Printed in U.S.A.

With a degree in mechanical engineering from Stanford University, the last thing **Melissa McClone** ever thought she would be doing was writing romance novels. But analyzing engines for a major U.S. airline just couldn't compete with her happily-ever-afters. When she isn't writing, caring for her three young children or doing laundry, Melissa loves to curl up on the couch with a cup of tea, her cats and a good book. She enjoys watching home-decorating shows to get ideas for her house—a 1939 cottage that is *slowly* being renovated. Melissa lives in Lake Oswego, Oregon, with her own real-life hero husband, two daughters, a son, two lovable but oh-so-spoiled indoor cats and a no-longer-stray outdoor kitty that decided to call the garage home. Melissa loves to hear from her readers. You can write to her at P.O. Box 63, Lake Oswego, OR 97034, USA, or contact her via her website, www.melissamcclone.com.

For everyone at cascadeclimbers.com. Without the forum, Hood Hamlet wouldn't exist, and I wouldn't have learned to climb!

Special thanks to: Karyn Barr, Kellie McBee, Fran Sharp, Terri Reed, Daniel Smith, Jennifer Rollins, Steve Rollins, Kevin McClone, Kurt Fickeisen, Jon Bell, Paul Soboleski, John Frieh, Mike Leming and all who helped out in my thread on the Climber's Board. Any mistakes and/or discrepancies are entirely my fault.

CHAPTER ONE

CHRISTIAN WELTON shoved his ski pole up the snow cave's air vent. He'd spent much of the night clearing snow from the shaft. Not that he was complaining. This cramped shelter on Mount Hood had saved his and his cousin's lives.

He glanced at Owen Slayter, who lay inside a sleeping bag. A foam pad kept the bottom of the bag dry from the snow beneath. The right side of Owen's face was swollen, bruised and cut. Dried blood coated his mouth. Superficial injuries.

Owen needed to be in the hospital with his multiple fractures. A helicopter rescue would be the fastest way off the mountain, but that hadn't been possible due to the weather.

Until help arrived, Christian would do whatever it took to keep them alive. That meant making sure Owen didn't go into shock or become hypothermic.

The inside temperature was approximately thirty-two degrees, practically balmy compared to the biting late-November cold. Christian listened, but couldn't hear anything outside the snow cave. He preferred the eerie quiet to the roar of wind as the storm unleashed its wrath yesterday.

For all he knew, Mother Nature had taken pity upon them, and the storm had passed overnight. A break in the weather would allow a rescue mission to be launched.

Time to find out if their luck had changed.

Christian slid off the raised sleeping platform. He wanted to see blue sky. He'd settle for gray as long as the wind and snowfall had died down.

At the entrance, he removed one of the backpacks covering the opening. Hope vanished in an instant.

Talk about an arctic hell. Seventy miles per hour winds, freezing temperature and zero visibility. He pushed aside the other backpack and peeked out. Each breath stung his lungs.

Disappointment shot straight to his cold toes. Helicopters wouldn't be flying today. No one would dare risk these conditions in the air or on foot.

Dammit. Christian's blood pressure rose to match his anxiety level.

Stupid dead cell phone battery. The thing was worthless. Useless. He hated not knowing what was going on down below or when help might arrive. If only…

Don't go there.

He had to concentrate on what was in his control. Anything else would only aggravate him more. Maybe upset him enough to make a bad decision.

Outside the cave, he struggled against the wind. He wiped snow from his neon-orange based skis—crossed in an X to mark the snow cave—so they would be visible to rescuers either from the air or ground should the weather suddenly improve.

Christian ducked inside the cave. He covered the entrance with the backpacks.

A chill shivered through him. His legs shook. He slapped his thighs with gloved hands.

What he wouldn't give for a steaming cup of hot cocoa right now. No whipped cream, but little marshmallows floating on the top.

Owen moaned.

Christian glanced at his cousin. Fantasizing wasn't going to get it done.

Time to melt some snow. Both he and Owen needed water to drink. Eating snow decreased body temperature and would allow hypothermia to set in quicker.

Carbon monoxide poisoning from using Owen's stove inside

the snow cave wasn't a big concern to Christian. Space between the packs, the vent and the wind outside allowed enough air movement and ventilation inside. But he still cleared the vent a couple times while the snow melted to make sure. He didn't want to take any chances.

With enough snow melted, he turned off the fuel then filled a water bottle. He climbed to where his cousin lay, careful not to sit too tall or he'd hit his head. Christian had been in such a rush to carve out the cave and get Owen out of the storm that he hadn't made the cave that big.

"Thirsty?" he asked.

As Owen blinked open his eyes, a grimace formed on his face. "Storm pass?"

His cousin's voice sounded hoarse, raw, like a wild animal. An injured, dying animal.

Christian's insides twisted.

Not dying. Owen was hurting. That was all. He'd groaned in pain through the night. Given his injuries a normal response. Both of them would get off this mountain and be climbing again. Not this season for Owen, but eventually he'd be back at it with Christian at his side. Or rather on his rope.

"The weather still sucks." Christian was a firefighter, used to running into burning buildings and saving people, not having to wait for someone to rescue him. He hated not being able to do more than keep his cousin warm and give him water to drink and energy bars to eat. "But people know where we are."

Owen cleared his throat. "OMSAR will find us."

He sounded stronger, confident they would be rescued.

Christian respected what OMSAR—Oregon Mountain Search and Rescue—did. Helping others when things went wrong appealed to him at a gut level. It was one reason he became a firefighter. He also loved being on a team where everyone watched each other's back and were equals.

Christian wasn't an equal of OMSAR. The mountain rescuer volunteers' skills far surpassed his own. He couldn't wait for them to arrive and get Owen out of here. But this storm would stop even the hardest of the hard men.

Still Christian knew Paulson and Thomas would get here when they could. They weren't only mountain rescuers, but firefighters. Part of the brotherhood. As soon as it was safe, they'd be here. No doubt Thomas would give Christian an earful, as usual. This time, however, he would gladly listen.

"Yes, they will," he said finally. Once the weather improved, OMSAR would know exactly where to locate them. Christian had given the 911 operator their GPS coordinates before his cell phone died. "Even if OMSAR doesn't make it up here today, we have all we need. Sleeping bag, bivy sacks, food, fuel for the stove and my wonderful bedside manner."

One side of Owen's dry and cut lips lifted in something that half resembled a smile. "You sound more like a mountaineer than a rock climber."

Christian straightened. His head brushed the ceiling. "That was the point of this climb."

"Then we succeeded." Owen had been climbing mountains since high school. Christian preferred rock climbing, but Owen thought it stupid to live on Mount Hood and not be able to climb it. Since spring, the two had climbed together throughout the Cascades. "I've always learned more from my failures."

"Then I should be an expert alpinist when we get down."

Owen laughed. Coughed.

Christian wished he could do more to help his cousin. Maybe there was something. When the rescuers arrived, they would need room to work. He reached for the shovel. "I'm going to make this place bigger. It's claustrophobic in here."

"Most snow caves are," Owen said. "Don't bother. You soaked through your clothes digging this out. You can't get your spare ones wet, too."

"If the snow settles—"

"We won't be here that long."

Christian wanted Owen to be right. At least he was more

alert. Talkative. Both were good signs after a restless and fit-
ful night.

A little tension released from Christian's tight shoulders.
"No worries. Remember, I'm one of Hood Hamlet Fire and
Rescue's finest. Strong. Brave."

"Full of it." Owen winced. He squeezed his eyes closed then
opened them slowly. "Save the firefighter shtick for the pretty
ladies. I got one word. Hypothermia."

"That would suck."

"Damn straight," Owen agreed. "If something happens to
you, there won't be anyone to brew water and feed me."

"Yeah, letting you go thirsty and starve wouldn't endear me
to your parents."

"Grandpa would be really mad at you, too."

Their grandfather, the patriarch of the Welton clan, would
never forgive him. Christian was persona non grata anyway
and would remain so until he moved home and embraced his
role at Welton Wineries. That wasn't going to happen because
of the terms his grandfather attached to whatever carrot he
dangled. If Christian ever returned, he wanted it to be on his
terms, no one else's.

He forced a smile. "Grandma wouldn't be too happy, either."

"And my sisters. And yours."

Owen's teasing was another good sign, but Christian couldn't
deny the truth in the words. He dropped the shovel. "Okay, I'll
wait."

Taking care of Owen was the most important thing Christian
could do. His family, especially his grandfather, might even
see that becoming a firefighter had been a smart decision. Not
simply a way to put off working at the winery.

"Thanks." Owen closed his eyes again. "Welton Winery
will go on now."

"Yeah." Their grandfather claimed the future of Welton
Winery rested in Christian's and Owen's hands. Never mind
Christian had other goals that didn't include just the winery
and living in the Willamette Valley. But family—make that his

grandfather's—expectations overruled individual dreams. Or so they were taught to believe. "Whether we want it or not."

Owen took a slow, deep breath.

Christian cleared the air vent again.

"Sorry for getting you into this." Owen sounded weaker once again.

"Hey, we're in this together." Christian had suggested they climb. His cousin had picked the objective. "No cutting the rope. No blaming each other. No losing it."

No matter how long they were stuck or how bad things got up here.

Things were bad up here. Driving winds limited visibility. The temperature remained in the low teens. The conditions weren't fit for man or beast.

Yet here she was.

Leanne Thomas sniffled, her nose runny from the cold temperature. Her breath sounded against the ski mask covering her face. A layer of ice covered her goggles and clothing. Ice probably covered her pack, filled with forty-odd pounds of gear and medical equipment.

But the only other place she wanted to be right now was higher on the mountain. At 10,500 feet to be exact. The approximate location of the two missing subjects. If only the rest of the six person OMSAR team would pick up the pace...

She gritted her teeth. This slower-than-snails pace up the south side of Mount Hood was killing her. Leanne wanted to climb faster, as part of a two-or-three-person hasty team, but Sean Hughes, the team leader, didn't want anyone to break a sweat and risk hypothermia. He could be such a mother hen during missions. The trait was both endearing and annoying.

The scent of sulfur from the Devil's Kitchen hung in the air. Not as bad as some days due to the wind. The hot fumes from the mountain kept the rocks free from snow, but she could barely see them today due to the conditions.

Okay, Leanne shouldn't diss Hughes. She understood his

concerns. Hypothermia and frostbite were real threats even with better conditions than yesterday. The lack of visibility meant they had to be especially cautious. No one wanted to lose a member of the team in this weather. But she hated having to move so darn slow knowing two climbers needed their help.

Worry gripped Leanne. Something she wasn't used to feeling on a mission. But this one was different than the others.

Focus, Thomas. Maintain objectivity.

Leanne jammed her ski pole into the snow. She'd been a mountain rescuer volunteer and a paramedic with Hood Hamlet Fire and Rescue long enough to know emotion didn't belong in the field. But staying detached wasn't so easy this time.

One of their own was missing.

Not an OMSAR member, but a Hood Hamlet firefighter. The station's rookie, even though he'd been working there for over a year now. The guy was the youngest among the professional firefighters at the station.

Christian Welton.

Leanne pictured his easy smile. Tall with brown hair and an athletic build, Welton defined the phrase babe-magnet with model-worthy good looks and striking blue eyes.

Not that she wanted to date him, or vice versa. Oh, he'd flirted with her at the beginning. His interest had surprised her. She discouraged the men she worked with so they would see her as one of them, not a woman. With Christian, that had been harder to do. But then he'd backed off, acting professional and treating her like the other guys. A good thing since the fire department frowned upon workplace romances.

But Welton was too hot for her not to notice him. She might not date anyone she worked with, but that didn't mean she couldn't look and appreciate a nice piece of eye candy on occasion. One who cooked a delicious Chicken Marsala and climbed, too.

He'd told her about learning to mountain climb, but rock

seemed to be more Welton's thing. Unless a bluebird powder day appeared. Then she'd bump into him skiing.

But the North Side of Mount Hood had some challenging, technical climbs. Not something a newbie should undertake. She'd never seen Christian act rashly before. She would be surprised to find out he had with this climb.

The temperature dropped. She ignored the biting cold and took another step. A gust of wind nearly knocked her over. She clutched her ski poles and regained her balance.

"Slow down, Thomas," Hughes shouted. "You're not on your own out here."

Leanne barely heard him over the wind. She slowed her pace. She was getting ahead of the others, but she hadn't felt this anxious since last Thanksgiving when a broken snowboard binding made Sean fall, injure himself and need rescue. One of the longest Thanksgiving days of her life.

Going after strangers was one thing, but someone she knew and worked with was a completely different situation. Over a year ago, Welton had strutted into the station full of confidence. He'd shown a sense of humor with the hazing and bad duty assignments. He'd also shown surprising competence and composure for a rookie. Though he could be annoying at times, Welton was dedicated. Hardworking. Too bad he didn't put as much effort into the women in his life.

Last night at the lodge, Leanne had gone up to a beautiful, but distraught young woman named Alexa and given her a candy bar. Alexa said she'd gone out with Welton a few times and was "a little" worried about him. Alexa seemed a bit more into him than she let on. Poor girl. Welton kept things light and casual with members of the opposite sex.

Leanne cleared her goggles with her gloved hand.

She knew more about the dating habits and marriages of the men she worked with than she wanted to know. But that knowledge helped her figure out what she wanted—and didn't want—in a relationship. She'd watched male friends, both firefighters and mountain rescuers, break women's hearts as if it were a hobby or game. She'd suffered too much heartbreak in her life to ever put herself in that position again.

The rescue team's slog up the mountain continued toward the Hogsback then east. She focused on each step.

Ice clung to her exterior clothing and accessories, but Leanne's base layer remained dry. She might be cold, but she wasn't freezing. Hughes deserved kudos for that.

He gathered the team together. "We're in range of the GPS coordinates. Look for markers. Anything to tell us where they might be."

As they searched, Hughes blew a whistle in hopes the missing men would hear it and make their whereabouts known. The sound carried better than a voice in this kind of weather.

If Welton and his cousin were inside a snow cave—which Leanne prayed they were—they might not be able to hear anything. The snow muted sounds. That made for peace and quiet during a storm, but could hamper rescue efforts if subjects didn't hear rescuers looking for them.

"X marks the spot," Paulson yelled, pointing to a pair of neon-orange bottomed skis marking a snow cave.

Relief washed over Leanne. Building a shelter was key to surviving out here in this kind of weather. She hurried over to the entrance. Backpacks covered the opening from the inside.

Paulson stood behind her. "Looks like the rookie knew what to do."

Leanne removed her pack and pulled out the medical kit. "Let's find out."

"Dude!"

Christian bolted upright from a sound sleep. He hit his head. The roof had settled more overnight. Soon the ceiling would be at their noses. "What?"

"They're here." Owen laughed as best he could. "They're finally here."

Adrenaline surged through Christian. Hallucinating was a symptom of shock and hypothermia. So not good.

Owen had been getting weaker and weaker, making Christian's anxiety level spiral upward. He did the only thing he could. He checked Owen's vitals. "Can you feel your feet?"

"I heard—"

One of the backpacks fell away from the snow cave entrance. The other followed. A red helmet poked inside. OMSAR.

Relief flowed through Christian's cold, sore body. Time to get Owen out of here.

"Yes," Owen whispered.

The rescuer crawled into the snow cave. He held a red duffel bag with a white cross on it. Ice covered his helmet, ski mask, goggles and black parka. The word RESCUE was written in white down one sleeve. He removed his goggles and pulled down his ski mask to expose his mouth.

Not a he. Christian's dry lips curved upward. "Thomas."

Leanne Thomas was a paramedic at the station. Pretty with an athletic, hot body. He'd wanted to ask her out when he first started working at the station, but she hadn't seemed as into him. He'd decided not to pursue her. A good thing, he'd learned. She wasn't his normal type.

Tough as nails and all business, Thomas was like a drill sergeant on steroids when it came to being out on a call or breaking in a rookie. She took her job seriously, expected others to do the same and never let her hair down. Christian wouldn't mind being around if she ever loosened that tight ponytail or those braids she wore.

Her face was pale except for her cheeks, flushed from the cold. She acknowledged him with a nod and sniffled. "Welton."

Surprising warmth flowed through him. His smile widened. "It's so good to see you."

"Good to see you, too, rookie." She removed her climbing gloves. "Paulson's outside. The chief's been letting us switch shifts so we could bring you home. No one wants to go back to eating Frank's Turkey Meatloaf Surprise for dinner."

Christian laughed. Something he hadn't done since yesterday. It really was good to see her. "I'll cook you whatever you want when we get down."

A smile tugged on the corners of her mouth. "Be careful, I might hold you to that."

She'd saved lives as a paramedic. She would help Owen. "Do."

Thomas pulled on exam gloves. "Injured? Feet?"

"Fine. Feet are cold, but I can feel my toes," he said quickly. "My partner—cousin—Owen fell skiing the face. He's twenty-six. No preexisting medical conditions. Looks like a broken ankle and arm. Some sort of knee injury."

"Hey, I'm right here." Owen sounded annoyed. That was much better than weak. "Conscious, in pain."

"I followed the NEXUS procedure to assess his spine before moving him in here," Christian added. "The threat of hypothermia and surviving the night outweighed spinal injury concerns."

"Good job, Welton," she said.

That was high praise coming from Thomas. He would gloat about it back at the station, but right now, he was relieved she hadn't spotted any problems with his care of his cousin.

As Thomas moved toward Owen, Christian tried to get out of her way. Not an easy feat in the cramped space.

She glanced around. "Did a hobbit design this place?"

"I was in a hurry," Christian admitted. "After two nights, the snow's settled a bit."

"Well, this cave kept you safe and warm. And you know what they say, size doesn't really matter." She winked at Christian, which caught him totally off guard, then she slid beside Owen. "Hello, Owen. Your cousin's been taking good care of you."

"You have such pretty brown eyes." Owen stared up at her as if she were Aphrodite. "Milk-chocolate with a hint of cream."

Christian stiffened. Owen must be in shock if he thought compliments would have an effect on Thomas. She wasn't interested in her looks. Not the way other women were. Sweet words wouldn't sway Thomas, either. She wasn't the flirty type. Christian had never met a more challenging or unapproachable woman in his entire life.

But she was strong and capable and here. That made her the most important person in the world at this moment. "My cousin is a chocolatier wannabe."

"I couldn't live without chocolate. Thank you, Owen." Thomas smiled softly, but her gaze focused in on his cuts and bruises. "I'm with OMSAR and a paramedic with Hood Hamlet Fire and Rescue. May I examine you?"

"Yeah." Owen glanced at Christian. "You never told me you worked with any women."

Christian tried hard not to think of her as a woman. "Thomas is one of the guys."

Owen scrunched his face. "You need your eyes examined, dude."

Thomas unzipped the sleeping bag, but kept Owen covered. "What your cousin means is all the men at the station consider me one of the guys. It's the same with the rescue unit."

Appreciation twinkled in Owen's eyes. "Idiots."

Thomas shrugged. "It's easier that way."

Christian found himself nodding, but he wondered if she meant easier on her or the men she worked with. He'd never given any thought to how being one of the guys might make Thomas feel. But then again, he'd never once seen her attempt to show her feminine side. She didn't fuss with makeup or jewelry.

As she examined his ankle, Owen winced. "Still idiots."

Christian stared at his cousin. "You realize you just called me an idiot."

"Yep," Owen said through clenched teeth. "Gotta side with the pretty paramedic in hopes she has pain meds in her bag."

Thomas's eyes twinkled, making her look prettier. "Oh, I have lots of good stuff in here."

"Knew it." Anticipation laced Owen's words.

Okay, so his cousin was flirting to get pain meds. Except...

Owen didn't need to charm medication out of Thomas. He would receive pain meds no matter what. He was flirting to flirt. Thomas didn't seem to mind, either. That was…strange.

Not that what his cousin did was any of his business. Thomas, either. But if anyone was going to get to flirt with her, it should be the guy still on his feet.

"Were you wearing climbing boots during your ski descent?" she asked Owen.

"Yeah," his cousin admitted. "Should have worn alpine touring boots. Should have done a few things differently."

"Failing upward was the right decision," Christian said.

Owen nodded, as Thomas continued her examination of him. "That domed cloud hovering like a UFO over the mountain didn't leave us a lot of choices."

Thomas looked at Owen. "Tough position to be in."

Owen raised one shoulder, the one attached to his good arm. "Climbing to the summit ridge and making a fast ski descent down the south side before visibility and conditions deteriorated completely would have worked if I hadn't fallen."

"Making ski turns in AT boots might have been easier, but you still could have fallen and broken your ankle." Thomas looked at Christian. "There's not enough room in here. Put your ski mask on, stick your head out and tell them to set up the tent if they aren't already doing it."

The cave felt too cramped and a little warm with three of them inside. He was definitely the odd man out.

"Welton."

What the hell was he doing just sitting here? Christian grabbed his ski mask. "On it."

CHAPTER TWO

WITH his face covered, Christian crawled out of the snow cave. The wind wasn't as strong as yesterday, but the visibility was still limited and the temperature freezing.

Bill Paulson, another firefighter from the station, stood next to the entrance with a large pack at his feet.

"Good to see you in one piece, Welton. Didn't want to have to break in another rookie. Doubt we'd find one who cooks as well as you." Paulson unscrewed the lid to a thermos bottle and handed it to him. "Drink this."

Christian pulled his ski mask below his mouth and sipped. Hot. Sweet. He'd been expecting plain water. "What is it?"

"The unit's special brew," Paulson said. "Jell-O mix and hot water. An odd combination, but what your body needs right now."

Speaking of needs… "Thomas wants the tent set up."

Paulson pointed to a group of rescuers struggling against the wind to erect the tent. "Hughes didn't think the snow cave would be big enough."

He must mean Sean Hughes, who owned a snowboard company and had married the gorgeous socialite Zoe Carrington this summer.

Christian didn't recognize the other men. The least he would do was lend a hand. "I can help."

"Yeah, you could, but warm up instead." Paulson motioned for him to drink more. "We might need your help getting the litter down the mountain if you're up for it."

Christian straightened. "Whatever you need."

"That's what I told Hughes you'd say," Paulson said. "Now get back in the snow cave until we're ready for you."

Christian crawled back inside with the thermos in hand. The interior was more claustrophobic after being outside for a few minutes. He pulled off his ski mask. His gaze went straight to where Thomas worked on Owen. An IV bag hung from the side of the snow cave alongside a headlamp.

"You've been busy," Christian said.

Thomas didn't glance his way, but concentrated on his cousin's splinted wrist. "Just doing my job."

A damn good job, too.

Thomas annoyed Christian by needing to cross every *T* and dot each *I,* but even then she impressed him. She didn't boast about her mountain rescue or climbing or paramedic skills. She did what was required and did it very well. For that he was grateful and now in her debt. He was going to owe the entire rescue team for getting him and Owen out of this mess.

Christian didn't like owing anyone. It rankled like a blister about to pop during the crux of a rock climb. He would have to think of something special to do for each one of them when they were off the mountain.

"I know it hurts." She spoke to Owen in a quiet, soothing voice. "But you'll start feeling better soon."

Owen basked in the attention and sweet bedside manner. Christian liked her soft tone better than the curt way she usually spoke at the station. He wouldn't be opposed to a little tender loving care from her.

Oh, wait. This was Thomas. Not going to happen unless he was a patient.

Paulson kneeled in the entrance. "Need anything, Thomas?"

She didn't look away from Owen. "Only the tent."

"It's going up." Paulson shifted his attention to Christian. "Your family's been at Timberline. Waiting. Praying. Nice folks."

A burst of emotion clogged Christian's throat. He might not

see eye to eye with his family, but he loved them. He swallowed. "Do they know you found us?"

"Hughes called it in," Paulson said. "Your family will be told then the media notified."

Christian's muscles tensed. "Media?"

"The mission call out brought a wave of press rushing to the mountain. The story went national yesterday afternoon. Headline news on all the cable channels and local newspapers," Paulson explained. "Two Oregon wine heirs missing on Mount Hood. Makes quite the public interest story."

Damn. Christian hadn't told anyone in Hood Hamlet about his family's successful winery in the Willamette Valley, three hours away. He wanted to be his own person, make his own way without his family's influence and interference. He'd learned at an early age help never came without strings attached.

"I don't blame you for not telling anyone about your family's winery," Thomas said. He was surprised she'd been paying attention since she seemed so focused on Owen. "I wouldn't have told anyone. Everyone would expect you to bring the wine to parties."

Once they were down, Christian would supply the entire rescue team with bottles of wine from his own winemaking hobby.

Paulson laughed. "Just like Porter and his beer."

Jake Porter owned the Wy'East Brewing Company and the Hood Hamlet Brew Pub. He was also a member of OMSAR and an all-around good guy. Christian enjoyed going to the brewpub. The entire town seemed to hang out there. "Is he with you?"

"He and Tim Moreno are on another rescue team. They'll meet us above Palmer where the Sno-Cat will be waiting," Paulson said. "Guys from the station have been stopping by the lodge. Bringing us food and coffee. Sitting with your family."

Christian appreciated the support. But that's what firefighters did for each other. A brotherhood of trust, loyalty and respect. He couldn't imagine not being a part of that. But after a year of being the rookie he knew exactly what would happen when he was back at the station. "They're never going to let me live this down."

"Nope," Paulson admitted. "At least not until someone else screws up bigger."

Christian grimaced.

"It's not that bad, Welton," Thomas said.

"Yeah," Paulson agreed. "It's not like you're a finalist for a Darwin Award."

Christian shuddered. So not something he wanted. The Darwin Award was given to people who killed themselves in stupid ways thus removing their DNA from the human gene pool.

Thomas laughed. The melodic sound filled the snow cave.

Christian had heard her laugh before, but he didn't remember it sounding like that.

"Oh, yeah, one of the guys with such a sweet laugh," Owen said with a big smile. The pain meds must be working.

But his words echoed Christian's thoughts. He liked the way her laugh sounded. Relaxed. Softer. Feminine. Maybe she wasn't as much a hard-ass as he thought.

He shook the crazy thought from his head. Nothing about Thomas was sugar and spice. Or remotely soft.

She joked with the guys at the station and could hold her own with the pranks that went on. He liked that about her.

"Don't let that laugh fool you. I've known Thomas since we were nine. She could kick all the boys' butts back then, too." Paulson grinned at Christian. "Meant to tell you, your girlfriend is at the lodge waiting for you, too."

Christian flinched. Girlfriend was a four-letter word. "I don't have a girlfriend."

"Alexa," Paulson clarified. "That girl is smokin'."

Oh, her. "Definitely, hot, but we just date. Nothing serious." Alexa was a great girl. Fun to be with. More fun to mess around with. Perfect because that was all he wanted right now. "She won't be around much longer with Christmas coming up."

"Is she going out of town?" Thomas asked.

"Come on, Thomas," Paulson teased. "You should know how it works by now. Holidays are the time for us good-looking guys to be footloose and fancy-free."

"Oh, no, Welton." Thomas sounded aghast. "Please don't tell me you're one of those guys who breaks up with women before Christmas."

"Okay, I won't tell you." Christian grinned. "But Paulson's right. The holidays only complicate relationships."

"Not to mention the hassle and expense of buying presents." Paulson had taken over as the resident heartbreaker in Hood Hamlet after the marriage bug bit Sean Hughes and Jake Porter. "Remember to break up with them before the second Monday in December or you're stuck."

Thomas's mouth gaped. "There's a December breakup deadline?"

Both Christian and Paulson nodded.

"That's so wrong." Thomas continued to work on Owen. "I've got to side with the women here."

"Idiots," Owen said in a singsong voice.

"I hope a woman never treats you guys like this," she said.

Christian usually ignored Thomas's disapproval, but this time it bothered him a little. Weird. "The women don't seem to mind when I swing back around a few days after the twenty-fifth."

She glanced up. "You go back to them afterward?"

Christian was surprised by her sympathy for the women he dated. Thomas kept her personal life private, but he'd seen her around town with guys. Just no one from the fire station. He'd thought she might be like him—only dating casually. He never thought she could be seriously involved with someone or looking to get involved.

None of his business, he reminded himself.

"Hey, I need someone to kiss when the clock strikes midnight on New Years," Christian said.

"Damn straight," Paulson agreed.

Christian wondered what it would be like to kiss Thomas. He'd bet she kissed as well as she did everything else.

"And sometimes," Paulson continued. "If you're lucky, you get a belated Christmas gift, too."

"I thought Hughes and Porter were players." Thomas checked Owen's vitals. "They had nothing on the two of you."

Paulson beamed like a kid with straight A's on his report card. "Thanks, Thomas."

"Yeah, thanks," Christian said.

Her eyes narrowed. The color resembled dark chocolate now. Her eyes looked prettier than usual, sexier.

She sighed. "That wasn't a compliment, boys."

Interesting. Why hadn't he noticed her eyes got very sexy when annoyed?

The rescue team brought Owen down the mountain in the litter. Leanne couldn't do anything more for him out in the elements so she assisted with the descent.

Snow swirled, but the temperature remained steady. That would make things easier on Welton.

Leanne glanced his way. He moved slowly, cautiously, as if he didn't want to make a mistake. A picture of perfect mountaineering technique.

"Almost there," she said.

Welton had to be exhausted, and even a little hypothermic.

She couldn't make out his features or see his eyes with all his winter gear and goggles on, but his shoulders hunched slightly. That couldn't be from the weight of his pack. The gear had been distributed among the rescue team.

A signal his condition had changed? Better find out. Welton would never complain. "You doing okay?"

"No different from when you asked five minutes ago," he answered. "My condition hasn't changed."

"If it had, would you tell me?"

"No."

The guy had the never-say-die attitude down pat. His willingness to want to assist in the descent after two nights in a snow cave impressed her. He showed strength and courage not found in a lot of people these days.

Whoa. She was sounding like a total Welton fangirl. That wasn't like her to go on and on about a guy. Time to get back to business. "We should see the Sno-Cat and the other rescue team any minute."

"Is that them?" His ski mask muffled his voice.

Jake Porter and Tim Moreno led the way with three other OMSAR members behind them. "Yes. That's Rescue Team 2. Fresh arms and legs will speed up the descent."

The sooner they arrived at the Sno-Cat, parked above the Palmer ski lift, the sooner they could get down to Timberline and out of the cold.

Welton moved closer to the litter. "If you'd let me help more—"

"You've done enough, Welton." She understood his frustration. Firefighters were trained to help. "In a few minutes, you'll be inside the Sno-Cat and riding down the hill. An ambulance will take you to the hospital."

"I don't need—"

"If you aren't checked out and cleared by a doctor, the chief will keep you off line duty." No one at the station wanted to be forced to sit out calls. "You've got to go."

Christian grumbled. "Are you going down in the 'Cat?"

"One of our unit members is a doc. He'll be with you. I'm skiing down with the team." As Welton's pace slowed more, her concern and unease rose. "You cold?"

"Just a little down." He exhaled on a sigh. The condensation from his breath hung on the air. "Wish I could ski with you guys."

His wistful tone tugged at her heart. She would much rather

ski than ride the loud, uncomfortable Sno-Cat. Skiing was faster, too. "Another day."

He straightened. "I might hold you to that."

Leanne grinned at the way he'd mimicked her words back at the snow cave. "Do."

"When?"

The guy had been through so much. She might not be able to see his smile, but she wanted to hear it in his voice. "Whenever you want to go."

The newest member of OMSAR, Dr. Cullen Gray, charged in front of Porter and Moreno.

"Thomas." He studied Owen, bundled up in the litter like a swaddled newborn, then looked at her. "That was a fast decent."

"Seemed a little slow to me. I hope you and the rest of the team kept warm." Gray had moved to Hood Hamlet this past summer. "Patient is twenty-six. Good health. Stable vitals. Multiple fractures of his left wrist and ankle. Possible ligament tear on the right knee. Facial lacerations."

"Morphine?" Gray asked.

She nodded. "All he'd had until we arrived was a couple ibuprofen."

The second team joined the others in lowering the litter.

"We gave him an initial five milligrams and another five due to his pain level and needing to get him down the mountain," Leanne continued. "His vitals remained stable after the meds."

"We'll get him into the Sno-Cat," Gray said. "What about the other subject?"

Leanne motioned to Welton. "Twenty-eight. Excellent health. A little hypothermic. Slight dehydration. Annoying at times."

She waited for Gray to respond. He didn't. And people called her too serious and intense.

"I'm fine, Thomas," Welton said.

Gray motioned to the Sno-Cat. "We'll make sure."

Welton glanced her way. She imagined a frown on his handsome face.

"Take it easy, Welton." She wanted to cheer him up. "Follow doctors orders. Don't break any nurses' hearts."

"I'll do my best." He sounded as if he might be smiling a little. "Anything else?"

"Yeah. Feel better."

"I never knew you cared, Thomas."

The tenderness in his voice made her heart bump. Leanne must be more tired than she realized if Welton could affect her that way. She squared her shoulders. "I don't. But my stomach appreciates your cooking."

With a laugh, he climbed into the Sno-Cat. The door slammed closed.

Another mission almost ready for the logbook. She stared at the Sno-Cat with a satisfied smile.

"Race you down," Paulson challenged, the way he had since they were nine and had met her first day at elementary school.

"You're so going to lose," Leanne said as usual.

"Yeah," Paulson admitted. "But I'll still be kicking back in the lodge way before the Sno-Cat arrives."

The Sno-Cat's engine revved. She wished Welton could be with them racing down the hill instead of riding in that thing. The guy deserved a break for taking such good care of his cousin. Maybe she should invite him…

"Before you hotshots head down," Sean Hughes said. "Don't forget the media will be waiting for us."

Leanne groaned. So did a couple other members on the team. Dealing with the press was her second-least favorite part of mountain rescue. Body recoveries were the first.

"Come on, now." Hughes looked at each one of them. "The press has a job to do. You know reporters won't go home without a story. They'll make up stuff and get it wrong if we don't answer their questions. Who'll talk to them with me?"

Apprehension coursed through Leanne's veins. The media circus got out of hand fast. She didn't want or need any attention for helping others in need. If she gained some good karma for her own climbing endeavors, okay. But if not, no biggie. "I pass."

Paulson gave her a nod. "I'll do it so Thomas can put her feet up and eat some bonbons before the debriefing."

Yeah, right. She smiled. "Have at it, boys. While you're showing the cameras your good side, I'll be sure to have a bonbon or two for each of you."

Leanne skied down the mountain. With the wind and snow on her, the cold seeped into her bones the way it had farther up the mountain. She couldn't wait to park herself in front of the day lodge's fireplace and warm up.

Fortunately skiing down didn't take much time at all.

The press stood waiting like hungry piranhas ready for a meal. Reporters jockeyed for the perfect position. Camera lights blared. People shouted questions. Others took photographs.

Leanne moved quickly past them in silence. She dumped her skis and poles in OMSAR's storage/catchall room. She also removed her rescue jacket. She didn't want any press who wandered inside bothering her.

She sat at one of the day lodge's tables and removed her ski mask, helmet and gloves. The scent of fresh-brewed coffee made her mouth water, but first things first.

Leanne removed her boots. Freedom! Her feet would have shrieked in delight if they could. She wiggled her cold toes.

A cup of steaming coffee appeared in front of her. "Nice work up there."

She looked up to see a former roommate. "Thanks, Zoe."

Zoe Hughes, Sean's wife, was an associate member of OMSAR. She was also the most beautiful woman in Hood Hamlet. Straight brown hair hung past her shoulders. She'd decide to give up her tabloid trademarked blond locks and go au naturel with her hair color. "Tired, Lee?"

"A little." Leanne sipped the coffee. The hot liquid tasted so good. "Sean's out with the press."

"Figured that's where he'd be." Zoe glanced toward the double doors. "My mother thinks he has a future in politics."

"What does Sean think?"

"I don't really want to repeat it."

Leanne laughed. She took another drink. "If I fall asleep, make sure someone wakes me for the debriefing."

"I will." With that Zoe floated away. Ever since marrying Sean her feet never seemed to touch the ground.

That blissful state was something Leanne had never experienced. She'd dated, a couple of times seriously, but she'd never felt that way about any man. Someday, Leanne hoped she would.

Her heavy eyelids drooped. Fatigue from the climb and rescue overtook her need to stay awake until the rest of the team came inside. She closed her eyes.

An unexpected image of Welton appeared, smiling at her the way he had in the snow cave. Up on the moutain, he'd made her feel like the most important person in the world. His word, at least. She yawned. Too bad that feeling had to end.

Exhaustion kept her eyes from springing open. The guy smiled a lot, but she couldn't remember the last time one had been directed at her. She'd liked how it felt then. She might as well enjoy his smile now.

Two days later, Leanne arrived at the Hood Hamlet Fire Station craving a sense of normalcy. No matter where she went in town yesterday on her day off, the rescue had been the topic of conversation. That annoyed her.

She entered the dining area. The scent of fresh-brewed coffee greeted her. Paulson handed her a cup that she accepted gladly. The perfect way to start her shift. Both B and C shifts crowded around the table. A few volunteers, too.

"Finally," Marc O'Ryan, her medic partner, said. "We want to hear all about Welton's rescue."

Oh, no. Leanne swallowed a sigh. She looked at each of the faces in the room. Only Welton was missing.

Bummer. She'd wanted to hear how Owen was doing. But she also wanted to see how Welton was faring. She'd thought about him lots yesterday. More than she would have expected.

"Before we hear about the rescue," the lieutenant announced, "let's get the morning briefing over with."

The exchange of information took less than five minutes. A new record.

"Now it's Paulson and Thomas's turn," the lieutenant said.

Leanne wanted no part of this. "I'm going to let Paulson tell you what happened. I've got some stuff to do with the toy drive."

Every year the fire station put on a toy drive to help local families in the area who were in need. Leanne usually ended up in charge. Not that she minded. It was a great cause.

"Go on," Paulson said. "I don't mind telling the tale."

Leanne left him to entertain the captive audience. She preferred putting missions behind her, no matter the outcome, not dwelling on them. Nothing good came from rehashing things over and over again. Life didn't give do-overs. No matter how much a person might want to change what happened, they couldn't. Learn whatever lessons there were and move on.

She grabbed a pair of scissors and the fire station's toy drive supply box. She rolled out two large barrels from the back room into one of the apparatus bays. Additional drop-off bins around town might increase the number of donations. Right now things weren't looking so good. Only two new toys had been dropped off. One was from her.

She measured the barrels with the roll of red-and-white striped wrapping paper. If she worked fast, she could have these decorated before the rest of the station came out to check the vehicles. She kneeled on the cement.

"Thomas."

Leanne recognized the voice immediately. Welton. She turned.

With an easy smile and bright eyes, Welton strode toward her in his uniform—a navy T-shirt and pants. His steel-toed shoes sounded against the pavement with a rhythmic clip. He moved with the grace of an athlete. Not bad for a guy who'd spent two nights in a snow cave. He'd shaved the stubble from his face. His light brown hair with an above the collar cut had been neatly styled. Quite a difference from his bad-boy look a couple days ago on the mountain.

Her heart went pitter-pat, a totally unexpected, unwelcome reaction. Okay, Welton was tough. He'd survived on the mountain and saved his cousin. That explained why her insides suddenly felt like goo. "You're the last person I expected to see today, rookie."

He stopped next to her. "Good morning, Thomas."

"Bet it feels like a great morning to you."

"Nothing like a comfy bed and a hot shower to make a person realize how good they have it."

"You're right about that." She lowered her gaze from his face. Uh-oh. She was eye level with his, um, pant's zipper. Heat rose up her neck. She faced the bins. "You missed the morning briefing."

"Chief put me on light duty and told me not to rush in."

Leanne bet it would be hard for Welton to watch the engine go out without him.

"He wants me to do some interviews here today," Welton continued. "Chief thought it might give the station and town a little PR."

She cut two large pieces from the wrapping paper. "Smart thinking. Hood Hamlet's been hurting with the drop in tourism. I've never seen so few donations to the toy drive."

"It's only the second of December."

"True, but usually we receive a lot of toys when the drive kicks off. If donations don't improve significantly, we won't have enough toys to match the number of requests we've received. There are a lot more needy families around here this year."

"No worries," Welton said. "All you need is a little Christmas magic."

Most of the old-timers around Hood Hamlet, and some of the not so old ones believed in Christmas magic. Leanne, not so much. Okay, not at all. She knew better than to put her faith in legends and fairy tales. Hard work and perseverance were the only things a person could count on. Even then life could change in an instant.

She returned the scissors to the supply box. "Oh, yeah, those barrels will be filled up with toys by the end of the week faster than I can say abracadabra."

"I never knew you were so cynical, Thomas."

"Not cynical," she countered. "Realistic."

"Being realistic isn't all that fun."

Welton's words didn't surprise her. She'd met his family at Timberline Lodge. Nice folks. Caring. Wealthy. He probably had never dealt with real disappointment his entire life. That was why he acted so carefree.

"Maybe not, but being realistic keeps you from crashing to earth as often." She positioned the wrapping paper around the first bin. "What the toy drive really needs is free publicity."

He held the paper against the barrel with his large hands. The hands of a climber with several small white scars and a larger one, as if he'd scraped off skin jamming his hand into a crack. "Let me help."

Welton moved closer. He smelled nothing like the mountain today. His fresh-soap-and-water scent surrounded Leanne with intoxicating maleness.

"Thanks." As she taped the bright paper around the bin, warmth emanated from him like a space heater set on high. "Any word on Owen this morning?"

"He's with the doctors at the moment," Welton said. "My aunt's going to text me when he's out."

"Keep me posted on his condition, okay?"

"Uh, sure."

He turned the barrel, making it easier for her to tape. As she scooted closer, her left shoulder brushed his right leg.

Heat burst through her at the point of contact. Leanne tensed and moved away from him.

What was going on? They'd worked closely before out on calls, but she seemed hypersensitive this morning. Concern over his well-being from the rescue hadn't gone away yet.

She added another piece of tape. "Finished with this one."

"It looks like a giant peppermint stick."

Leanne nodded. "All I need is ribbon and a boy."

"A boy?" The humor in Welton's eyes echoed in his voice. "Is that what you want Santa to bring you, Thomas?"

Her cheeks warmed. Being around him made her feel self-conscious, tongue-tied. So unlike herself. "I meant a bow."

"Boys are more fun," he teased.

She reached for the other piece of wrapping paper to cover the second barrel. "Except those who don't want a girlfriend for Christmas."

"Hey, I'm lots of fun."

"Not from where I'm standing."

"You're kneeling."

"Go bother someone else."

"You get that honor this morning, Thomas." He took the sheet out of her hands. "You tape. I hold."

Leanne preferred doing things on her own. Well, not climbing. A partner came in handy then. Still, having an extra set of hands to wrap these barrels was…helpful. "Be careful, if you keep this up, you may find yourself on the committee."

He positioned the paper. "Committee?"

Leanne tore off a piece of tape. "The toy drive committee."

"There's a committee?"

"Me, myself and I." She taped the paper in place. "But I have lots of helpers."

"I'm more of a helper type than a committee person."

"Most guys are." Leanne placed the tape in the supply box. "If donations come in, I'll need a few strong men with trucks."

"Now it's men with trucks." An irresistibly charming grin lit up his face. "Santa's got his work cut out with you."

Leanne picked up the roll of red ribbon and wrapped it around the first barrel. "I'm actually pretty easy…"

Welton's eyebrows shot up.

"…where Santa is concerned," she finished.

CHAPTER THREE

LEANNE tied a neat bow around the first barrel then decorated the second one. "All done."

Christian nodded. "Now it's my turn."

The blue of his uniform deepened the color of his eyes. She wished she hadn't noticed that. "What do you mean?"

Her voice came out harsher than she intended, but something about Welton was messing with her senses. Her brain. Her hormones. She didn't like it.

"Things were so crazy yesterday when we arrived at the Sno-Cat, I never said thank you," he said. "I appreciate all you did up there, Thomas. The rest of the team, too."

"You're welcome. Next time—"

"There isn't going to be a next time," he interrupted. "Not if I can help it."

"Right answer, rookie."

He smiled at her.

She smiled back.

Time seemed to stop. Something passed between them.

Gratitude. That was all it was. On both their parts.

Yet his gaze lingered, as if there was something more.

Leanne looked at the wrapping paper lying on the ground.

This was Welton for goodness' sake. Sure, he was a capable, sexy guy, reliable even for a rookie, but not when it came to romance. If she were dating him, she wouldn't be satisfied with just a date, just fun. She'd want all of him.

Not that she was in the market for a romance, Leanne reminded herself. She was taking a break from the dating scene.

She placed the red ribbon into the supply box. "I need to clean up before the news crew shows up."

"Yeah, I don't want anything to get in the way of my fifteen minutes of fame," Welton teased.

"I'm sure you'll have a legion of fans by the time the fifteen minutes are over."

"A compliment?"

"Maybe."

His smile widened. "I'll take it."

Quite the charmer. She didn't know whether to envy the women he dated or feel sorry for them.

"I'm going to pay you back for everything you did yesterday," Christian said.

"Not necessary."

He shrugged, looking unconvinced. "The least I can do is share the spotlight today."

Her stomach clenched. "Really not necessary."

"It is," Welton admitted. "Chief wants you and Paulson to be part of the interviews if you're not out on calls."

Oh, no. Her heart sank to the tip of her steel-toed zip-up boots. "Interviews aren't my thing."

"Come on," Welton encouraged. "Someone like you can't be camera shy."

Someone like her. One of the guys. But the guys didn't know everything about her. She wanted to keep it that way.

Leanne shrugged, but she didn't feel indifferent. She'd put the past behind her, but she hadn't forgotten everything. She couldn't. Her life had been changed in an instant, but the media hadn't cared. They'd only wanted the story, the inside scoop. No matter what it had taken to get the information.

She shivered at the memory.

Christian touched her shoulder. "Cold?"

Leanne shrugged away from his hand. Straightened. She didn't like appearing weak. To others or herself. "I'm fine."

"You don't look fine."

She pressed her lips together. "I am."

Welton didn't look convinced.

Odd. Most of the guys around here took Leanne at her word. "Really."

His assessing gaze suggested Welton didn't believe her. His perceptiveness over her uneasiness and his seeming to care how she felt disconcerted her.

"Hello." A beautiful blond woman entered the station. Her high-heeled boots clicked against the floor. Two men, carrying bags and camera equipment, followed. The scent of her jasmine perfume wafted through the air. "I'm Rachel Murray with the Portland Evening News."

Leanne stood. She wiped her sweaty palms on the thighs of her pants then shook the woman's hand. "Leanne Thomas."

Rachel's straight teeth gleamed as if they'd been recently whitened. "I just interviewed your rescue team leader, Sean Hughes. He had wonderful things to say about you. Not only as a paramedic, but one of the best and fastest climbers with OMSAR."

Leanne shifted her weight. "Thanks."

Rachel turned her attention to Welton. "And you're Christian Welton. I'd recognize you anywhere."

He shook her hand. "Nice to meet you, Rachel. Thanks for coming all the way from Portland."

She didn't release his hand. "It's our pleasure. I'm sure you've been inundated with interview requests."

Christian pulled his arm away. "A few."

"I was told another member of the rescue team works here, too," Rachel said.

He nodded. "Bill Paulson. He's around here somewhere."

"Why don't you get set up," Rachel told her crew, who went to work. As she looked around, her gaze zeroed in on the red-and-white toy barrels. "Those look Christmassy. What are they for?"

"Drop-off bins. The fire station runs an annual toy drive for

needy children in Hood Hamlet and the surrounding areas."
Leanne didn't like talking to the media, but she would for the
toy drive's sake. "Unfortunately donations are down this year."

"That's too bad," Rachel said.

Leanne nodded. "I'm hoping more toys come in soon."

As Rachel shrugged off her wool coat, Welton lent a hand.
Interesting. Leanne had never noticed his manners before.
Or maybe he wanted to hook up with the pretty reporter. He
had a little time left until the December breakup deadline.

"Hey, I have an idea." The slow, seductive smile spreading
across Welton's face told Leanne she'd nailed the motivation
behind his gentlemanly behavior. "Any chance you could mention the toy drive on camera, Rachel?"

Okay, that was unexpected. Leanne hadn't thought he'd been
paying attention to what she'd said, or cared.

Rachel wet her glossed lips. "Are you involved in the toy
drive, Christian?"

"He's been a big help," Leanne answered for him. She wasn't
about to blow this opportunity.

"I helped decorate the barrels," he said.

"Really?" Rachel sounded intrigued.

Welton gazed into the reporter's eyes as if she were the only
woman in the world. And he the only man.

A lump formed in Leanne's throat. Not one man had ever
looked at her that way. She imagined it would feel pretty ter-
rific.

"Every kid should have a present to open on Christmas."
Welton's gaze remained on Rachel. "I'd appreciate anything
you could say about it. So would Leanne. She heads the committee."

"Oh, you're on the committee, Christian," Rachel assumed
wrongly. "That's wonderful."

He looked uncomfortable. "Anything for the kids."

Rachel leaned toward him. A combination of eagerness and
attraction gleamed in her eyes. "I'd be happy to say something.
Publicity could spur donations and help your committee."

His committee. Leanne bit back a smile. She would make Welton an honorary member so he wouldn't be stretching the truth too much.

"That would be great." He pushed a stray strand of hair off Rachel's face. "There now I can see your pretty eyes better."

The reporter released a swoon-worthy sigh. "Thanks."

"Thank you," he said.

Leanne watched the exchange with interest. Welton impressed her. Being a player had its advantages.

"You know what," Rachel said to Welton as if Leanne wasn't there. "I'll talk to a friend at the newspaper and a couple of Portland bloggers about the toy drive, too."

He grinned. "The more the merrier."

Oh, he was good. Highly skilled in the art of seduction, no doubt. If that was what it took to fill the drop-off bins with toys, so be it. Still Leanne felt sorry for Rachel Murray.

The poor reporter had just fallen for Welton. Hard. But what woman wouldn't with him pouring on the charm like that. Rachel would be disappointed if she expected a holiday romance to develop. Though maybe she would be the one Christian kissed on New Year's Eve.

The thought left Leanne a little unsettled. She shook it off.

"We're ready," the cameraman said.

Rachel smoothed her skirt. "Why don't one of you grab Bill Paulson, and we can get started with the interview?"

"You up for it, Thomas?" Christian asked.

Leanne knew he wasn't talking about getting Paulson. The Portland Evening News broadcasted across Oregon and Southwest Washington. If Rachel Murray was willing to give the toy drive a plug and up the chances of children in need getting a present for Christmas, an interview was the least Leanne could do. Even if it was the last thing she wanted to do.

She took a resigned breath. "Yeah, Welton. I'm up for it. I'll get Paulson and be right back."

* * *

Rachel Murray was hot. Exactly Christian's type.

Her perfectly-applied makeup accentuated pretty, elegant features. His hands itched to run through her mane of blond hair. Her killer body would look better naked. She'd also asked reasonably intelligent questions these past five minutes. Beauty, brains and breasts—a perfect combination.

So why was he more interested in how nervous Thomas looked right now than the sexy reporter?

Christian always tried to pretend Thomas wasn't a woman, but today, he couldn't. She seemed almost vulnerable, spurring his protective instincts.

"Anything you wish you would have had with you in the snow cave, Christian?" Rachel asked.

"A better first aid kit and a charged cell phone would have come in handy. More food, too." He felt a little embarrassed about having to be rescued. "Otherwise, we were good."

Rachel turned her attention to Thomas. "Rescues in this time of year don't always turn out this well, do they, Leanne?"

"No, they don't," Thomas agreed. "Three climbers lost their lives in December 2009. Three more back in 2006."

She might be nervous, but she was hanging in there. Christian respected that, respected her.

"Wasn't there an OMSAR member who also died in a winter climbing accident?" Rachel asked.

Thomas's features tightened. She nodded once.

"Yes." Bill Paulson took over without missing a beat, but his tone sounded strained. "Nick Bishop, a member of OMSAR, and Iain Garfield, a talented, young alpinist, died a few days before Christmas eight years ago."

Christian hadn't heard about these two climbers before, but they'd obviously impacted both Thomas and Paulson.

"Very sad," Rachel empathized. "How does knowing others died while you and your cousin, Owen, survived make you feel?"

"Thankful," Christian said truthfully. "Grateful. Lucky."

"Do you think anything other than luck was involved in the rescue, Leanne?" Rachel asked.

"Christian and Owen had the skills to build a shelter to protect them from the environment and the proper gear to keep them warm, hydrated and fed until help could arrive," Thomas said. "Those things go a long way to ensuring a good outcome."

She'd never ever used Christian's first name before. It sounded…strange. He was used to her calling him Welton, as the other guys at the station did.

"Even with right equipment and proper training, nothing is ever guaranteed," Bill added. "A little luck and good karma always come in handy on the mountain."

"What about Christmas magic?" Rachel asked.

Thomas inhaled sharply. A sideways glance passed between her and Paulson.

"Sean Hughes said a little Christmas magic could have contributed to the rescue's happy ending," Rachel continued. "What do you think about that, Leanne?"

Christian straightened. She wasn't the person to answer this question.

"Everyone in Hood Hamlet seems to have an opinion about Christmas magic," Thomas stated without any emotion in her voice. "Whatever the reasons behind the mission's success, we're all happy Christian and his cousin are safe."

"Your opinion, Bill?" Rachel asked.

"A lot of things that could have easily gone wrong up there didn't," Paulson said. "Owen had no spinal or head injuries. The cell phone battery didn't die until the GPS coordinates had been given to the 911 operator. The weather broke long enough so we could head up the mountain and bring them down. Seems a bit more was involved than simply dumb luck."

Thomas pressed her lips together. Her eyes darkened, but not to that deep, sexy chocolate color from yesterday.

Something was bringing her down. She looked sad, as if she were hurting. Christian didn't understand why, and he fought the urge to reach out to her.

"You were the one stuck in the snow cave for two nights, Christian," Rachel said. "Do you think Christmas magic helped you and Owen get off the mountain alive?"

He shifted his gaze from Thomas to the reporter. "Finding yourself in a situation with everything out of your control, you get religious fast. Making deals and promises you know you can't keep," he admitted. "I have to agree with Sean and Bill. It seems like something more was going on up there. I've only lived in Hood Hamlet a little over a year. But if the dedicated members of OMSAR want to call it Christmas magic, so will I."

"There you have it. Christmas Magic on the Mountain." Rachel beamed. "Christian and Leanne are members of the Hood Hamlet Fire Department's Christmas Toy Drive committee. Why don't you help them drum up some magic of their own by donating a new, unwrapped toy and make a needy child's Christmas morning a little brighter? Drop-off barrels are located here at the fire station. This is Rachel Murray for the Portland Evening News in the quaint Alpine village of Hood Hamlet."

The light on the camera went off. The news crew put away their gear.

Damn. Christian had been called out on camera as a member of the toy drive committee. No way of getting out of that now.

"Great interview," Rachel said.

"I appreciate the plug about the toy drive," Leanne said, then walked away.

"Yeah, thanks," he agreed. "Very nice of you."

"My pleasure." Rachel smiled at him. "I'm happy to help."

He heard a familiar laugh. Thomas spoke with the cameraman—a tall guy with a beard. She laughed again. He did, too.

Christian rocked back on his heels. The cameraman was definitely interested in Thomas. Flirting. The guy's gaze practically devoured her.

First Owen. Now this guy. What was going on?

"I'll give you my number in case you need anything," Rachel said.

Christian turned his attention to the reporter. The way she batted her eyelashes emphasized the amount of mascara she wore. So different from…

He glanced at Thomas. She'd stopped talking to the cameraman. Had the guy asked her out? Christian hoped not. She could do better.

"Christian?" Rachel asked.

"I'd like your number." He would take her out for plugging the toy drive even though she'd landed him a spot on Thomas's committee. "Let me see your phone."

Rachel handed him a fancy smart phone protected in a silver-and-turquoise hard case.

He texted himself and handed her back the phone. "Now you have my number. And I have yours."

"Use it, okay?" She and her crew left the fire station.

"That went well," Christian said to his coworkers.

"She's hot." Paulson raised a brow. "Did you get her number?"

As Christian nodded, Thomas shot Welton an aggravated look. Interesting. Maybe she was jealous.

"Come on, guys." Frustration laced her words. "Christmas magic?"

Okay, not jealous, Welton realized with a twinge of regret.

"Hughes said it," Paulson countered.

She grimaced. "Hughes is infamous for his sound bites."

"Well, I wasn't about to disagree with our team leader on camera," Paulson said. "Besides, I believe it."

Thomas sighed loudly. "Christmas magic isn't real. If it existed, bad things wouldn't happen up here on Christmas."

"I'm bowing out of this conversation." As Paulson walked toward the station's living area, he glanced back. "If you're smart, Welton, you'll do the same."

Christian brushed aside the words. He wasn't about to let

this drop. "I thought Sean Hughes had the reputation of being a Grinch in this town, not you."

"Sean gave the appearance of being a Grinch before he met Zoe, but he would do anything for anybody," Thomas said. "And I never said anything about not liking Christmas. I just don't believe in magic."

Yesterday, her red cheeks, runny nose and sweet laughter had made her seem a little more…human. The vulnerability he'd glimpsed during the interview only added to that. Now she was back to being the same old hard-nosed Thomas. He preferred the other one. "What do you believe in?"

She raised her chin. "Being prepared, having the right skills and equipment, never getting in over your head."

"Sounds like something from an OMSAR training manual."

"It is."

"Then it's what OMSAR believes, not you."

"Wrong, rookie," she said. "I wrote the manual."

He shouldn't have been surprised. She probably approached being a mountain rescuer the same way as she did being a paramedic—by the book. "Well, if Christmas magic fills up those toy bins, you'll be changing your tune soon enough."

"Publicity and generosity will fill the bins. Nothing else."

"How will you know the difference?" he asked.

She picked up the supply box. "How will you?"

A beat passed. And another.

Stalemate. But he'd always known how tough Thomas was. The woman must have ice running through her veins. No matter how ugly it got on a call, she showed no emotion.

His gaze fell to her mouth. No lipstick. Not even a hint of lip gloss.

Christian wondered how she'd react if he kissed her.

Whoa. Thomas would deck him if he did that. He would deserve it for kissing her at the station. He needed to focus. "When's the next toy drive committee meeting?"

"I know that's not what you want," Thomas said. "You can be an honorary member of the committee."

"Thanks, but you heard Rachel. She said I'm on the committee. I need to be on it."

"No one will know."

"I will."

Lines creased Thomas's forehead. "You haven't shown any interest in the toy drive before."

"True." Christian never got too involved. He wanted only responsibilities he'd chosen for himself. "This is different."

Helping with the toy drive would be a great way to do something nice for Thomas. He'd teased her about what she wanted for Christmas, but he knew—a present for every child on the toy drive's list. She wouldn't stop working until she had enough donations. He could take some of that burden from her.

"I want to be on the committee this year," he said firmly.

Panic flashed in her eyes. "You can't be serious."

The überconfidence she usually exuded seemed to have disappeared. She seemed a little…disturbed. Good, because she was making him feel the same way.

"I'm very serious." Being on the committee wasn't only about repaying her for what she'd done on the mountain. Ever since the rescue, being around Thomas left him feeling unsettled. He didn't like that. Working with her on the toy drive would allow him to take control of the situation and conquer that feeling. "You'd better get used to the idea because you're stuck with me."

CHAPTER FOUR

Two days later, Christian parked at the curb in front of Thomas's three-story town house. The Craftsman-style architecture with wood beams and paned windows gave the neighborhood a quaint, mountain village feel. Towering, snow-laden Douglas fir trees stood behind the row of homes, but the neighborhood was walking distance to Main Street.

Snowflakes landed on his windshield. He turned off the ignition.

The single-car garage door of Thomas's house was open. Inside, three large green rubber bins with red lids sat in front of an all-wheel-drive Subaru wagon. An extension ladder rested against the front of the house. Near the top rung stood Thomas, stringing Christmas lights along the edge of the peaked roofline.

A single brown braid hung out the back of her red fleece hat. Her oversize navy jacket fell past her hips. Her black waterproof pants were tucked into a pair of snow boots. Her clothing suggested extreme weather, not a light snowfall. A storm hadn't been predicted, but the sky darkened.

He laughed.

Leave it to Thomas to predict the weather better than the meteorologists. Paulson had told him many local climbers talked to her before heading up the mountain, especially in the winter. Next time Christian would talk to her himself. Accidents happened, but he didn't want to put himself in another situation needing rescue. Once was more than enough.

Larger snowflakes accumulated on the hood of Christian's truck. He stayed in the cab, but not because of the weather.

Thirty minutes ago coming to talk to Thomas about the toy drive had seemed like a great idea. Now that he was here…

He tapped his thumbs against the leather-covered steering wheel. She might not want to be disturbed on a day off.

But leaving didn't appeal to him. Christian didn't want to wait another day until they were back at the station to talk to her. He'd been thinking about Thomas a lot since the end of their shift yesterday. He wanted to see her now.

Christian craned his neck to get a better look at her.

With one foot on the ladder and the other on the roof, she adjusted a portion of the lights. She showed no hesitation or the slightest wobble in her seamless movements. She returned her foot to the ladder as if she were standing on the ground and not a couple stories up.

Fearless. That was Thomas.

What the hell was he doing sitting here?

That *was* Thomas up there.

This wasn't a man-woman thing. He'd given up flirting with her over a year ago after seeing how gung-ho-by-the-book she was at the station. She wouldn't care if he dropped by unannounced. Christian needed to stop fooling around and get it done.

He slid out of his truck then shut the driver's door. If she agreed his plan was a good one—and how could she not?— he could pay back the entire rescue team members and all of OMSAR. Maybe he'd even put a smile back on Thomas's face.

As he walked up the driveway, his boots sunk into the snow. "Hey, Thomas."

She glanced down. Her brown eyes widened with surprise, then clouded with concern. Her mouth tightened. "Is Owen—?"

"He's recovering."

Thomas blew out a breath. The condensation hung on the cold air like a puff of smoke. "Good, for a moment I thought he'd taken a turn for the worse."

Christian appreciated her concern and was a little relieved she hadn't been keeping track of his cousin's progress herself. "Nope, Owen should be released from the hospital tomorrow."

"Good news."

"Yes." Christian studied her. Flushed cheeks. Runny nose. Stray tendrils peeked out the brim of her hat. Not primped, but fresh-faced and natural. Pretty.

"So what brings you by on your day off?" she asked.

"I have an idea about the toy drive."

Thomas adjusted a vertical strand of white icicle lights. "You want to talk about the toy drive now?"

"I can wait until you're finished hanging the lights."

"Okay," she said after a long moment. "This shouldn't take me more than a few minutes."

"Want help?" he offered.

She attached the cord to another hook. "Thanks, but I've got it."

Christian wondered how long she'd been decorating. He walked toward the front door. She'd gone all out.

Lights surrounded a large window on the second story, two smaller windows on the third level, the single-car garage door on the ground floor and the front door where a pine wreath with holly berries, pinecones and a big red bow hung. A single candle lamp sat on the inside pane of each window. A plastic snowman holding a broom stood on the porch, ready to greet visitors.

Thomas must like Christmas to go to this much trouble. Good. She would like his idea. Christian smiled.

A noise drew his attention. She stretched to the left to reach the last hook. The ladder shifted, the top scraping across the house.

Adrenaline surged through Christian. He reached for the ladder but missed it by mere inches. "No!"

"Oh," she cried.

Everything happened in slow motion. The ladder fell like a

tree, careening down until it crashed against the covered porch of the town house next door.

Christian positioned himself below Thomas, ready to break her fall. He braced himself. Except...

She didn't fall. Her feet dangled in the air while she hung from the roof.

His heart pounded. He struggled to breathe. She hadn't hit the ground, but she still could be hurt. "Leanne, you okay?"

"Yeah." She sounded disappointed, not frightened. "I only had one hook to go. I hope the ladder didn't hit you on the way down."

"It didn't." He hadn't thought about the ladder hitting him, only her taking a header and going splat on the driveway. The image still left him shaken. Partners had taken screamers—long falls—rock climbing. He'd fallen himself. Not a pleasant experience.

He stared up at her. "You anchored?"

"Of course. I installed bolts for this very reason." Thomas sounded annoyed he'd questioned her. "A fall from up here would break a lot of bones or kill me."

No kidding. Christian tried to calm the shallow breathing. A strange reaction considering the horrors he saw daily in his job. "I know."

She should have let him help her finish putting up the lights when he offered.

"You look a little pale, Welton." Concern laced each of her words. "Are you okay?"

Says the woman swinging almost three stories in the air. Most of the girls he knew would be screaming and crying, not worried about him. Talk about nerves of steel. His jaw tensed. "Come down now."

"Get the ladder."

Christian didn't move. She always seemed so in control and capable. He liked having the upper hand with her. "What would you do if I wasn't here?"

She pursed her lips. "I have my cell phone."

Of course she did. Thomas was prepared for anything whether at home or in the mountains.

"I'd call a neighbor or friend to come over," she continued.

"A good thing I'm here."

"Not if you leave me hanging up here much longer."

Point taken. Christian placed the ladder against the house and held on to it. "Come down."

"After I hook this last one."

"Leave it," he said.

"I want the lights to look nice."

"They're good."

"I want them to look great."

As she stretched to reach the final hook, he tightened his grip on the ladder. He wasn't taking any chances of her falling again.

She straightened. "There."

"I've got hold of the ladder."

"Not necessary, rookie."

"Humor me."

Thomas unclipped from the bolt. She climbed down as if the ladder were part of a bunk bed set. Both feet hit the ground. Now he could relax.

She removed her harness.

He studied her. "Sure you're okay?"

"I'm fine. Glad the fall wasn't any longer." With a smile, she folded up her harness. "That might have hurt a little."

A little? A smile tugged at Christian's lips. Okay, he liked her attitude. She would kick his butt climbing in the mountains, but he could hold his own on rock. "You rock climb?"

Thomas nodded. "I lead 5.10 and follow 5.11."

Awesome. They'd be able to hit a lot of fun routes in those grades. "Let's go to Smith Rock sometime."

Her mouth quirked. "You want to climb with me?"

"Yeah." Christian loved climbing with women. Not only were they prettier and smelled better than male partners, but nothing was sexier than a woman dancing up a wall of rock with amazing technique. He wanted to see how Thomas moved. Plus she seemed as if she would be a low-maintenance partner, one who carried her own weight, literally and figuratively, and wouldn't complain. "If you're up for it," he added, not wanting to appear too eager.

"I'm up for it." She tilted her chin. "Paulson told me you're quite the rope gun."

Christian tended to lead more routes than he followed, but he didn't mind switching off the sharp end of the rope. "Don't worry. I'll let you have a turn."

She gave him a long, hard look, making him feel as if he were on display. Thomas had never done that before. It made him feel good.

"That's generous of you." She motioned him toward the garage. "Let's get a coffee and talk about the toy drive."

Oh, yeah. The toy drive. That was the reason he'd come to see her.

Christian followed her into the garage. A minigym had been set up in the back with a pull-up bar, free weights and rowing machine. They entered the town house and went up a staircase.

He appreciated the earth tones and casual decor in the living area. The large couch, coffee table and chair looked comfortable. A purple throw lay across the back of the chair.

A river rock fireplace drew his attention. A large photograph of Mount Hood sat on the wood mantel. "Nice place."

"I like it," she said. "Some people rent to tourists, but enough of us live here full-time to give the development a sense of community."

Her words surprised Christian. She was so outdoorsy and independent. A secluded cabin built on land leased from the Forest Service seemed more her style than a town house that shared common walls and had a neighborly feel.

"All your decorations are up outside, but where's your Christmas tree?" he asked.

"I plan to get one today."

Christian studied the photographs on the walls. Mountain

landscapes. One black-and-white picture had a lone climber walking along a ridgeline. "Amazing photos."

"Thanks." She passed another staircase leading up to the third floor and a black wood dining table with a cherry top surrounded by six coordinating chairs. "I love being able to capture shots like that."

He looked at the picture then back at her. "You're a photographer?"

"A photographer wannabe." In the kitchen, she removed two coffee mugs from a cupboard, filled them with coffee from a pot on the counter then placed them on the breakfast bar. "I'm still learning, but I needed something to put on the walls. My former roommate used to display her snowboard designs. Those added a lot of color."

That roommate, a total snowboarding babe, had moved away right after he'd started working at the station. Paulson had been upset when she left for Vermont.

Christian sat on a stool at the breakfast bar. "Cocoa Marsh, right?"

"Yes, but she's Cocoa Billings now."

A wistful expression crossed Thomas's face. A look he wasn't used to seeing on her. She always seemed so…practical. In control. But she was lonely. A way he never expected her to feel. "You miss Cocoa."

Thomas nodded. "We lived together for over three. Way more good times, than bad."

"Hard to replace a friend like that."

"Yes." Thomas opened another cupboard, took out a bag and placed muffins on a plate. "Though, I didn't do too badly replacing Cocoa as a roommate. Zoe Carrington moved in last January and lived here until she married Sean in June."

That had been six months ago. Christian didn't see another car or tire tracks on the snow, but that didn't mean she lived alone. Or with another female. He leaned toward her. "Who's your roommate now?"

"No one." She placed the plate of muffins on the bar and

sat on the stool next to him. "I should try to find somebody. Hood Hamlet is a safe town, but I like knowing someone is here when I'm at the station."

Hood Hamlet's career firefighters and paramedics worked rotating shifts. Twenty-four hours on, forty-eight hours off. Volunteer firefighters had their own schedules.

He sipped the coffee. Strong and hot. "It must be nice to have the place to yourself when you're off."

She nodded. "But I don't mind having a roommate. Sure helps with the mortgage payment and utility bills."

Christian wouldn't know about a mortgage payment. Renting a room in a house with two guys from the fire station suited him fine right now.

He looked at the plate of muffins. Lots of choices. Blueberry, chocolate chip, cranberry and banana-nut.

"Help yourself," Thomas said.

He took a blueberry muffin and bit into it. Delicious.

Thomas took a chocolate chip one. "So what about the toy drive?"

Christian washed down the muffin with a sip of coffee. "I had dinner with Rachel Murray last night."

"You went out with the reporter?"

He nodded. "It was the least I could do after the plug she gave the toy drive."

"So the December deadline…"

Interesting. She remembered his dating ritual. Not that last night had been anything other than dinner. Unusual, but he hadn't felt like taking Rachel up on her offer to come in when he drove her home.

"Still in effect." He already had Alexa to cut loose. Getting involved with another woman didn't make a lot of sense. That must be the reason he'd left Rachel with only a good-night kiss. "Last night was a thank-you dinner. Nothing more."

"Really?" Thomas sounded surprised. Okay, doubtful.

Christian didn't blame her. Thank-you dinners weren't his usual MO. But even though Rachel was more his type, he couldn't stop comparing her to Thomas last night. The reporter had come up way short. "Yeah, really."

Thomas raised her mug in salute. "That was nice of you."

"Simply repaying a favor." As he wanted to do with her. He took another sip of coffee. "Rachel said there's been a lot of buzz surrounding our interview. I started thinking—"

"A dangerous thing."

He smiled. "I thought of a way to capitalize on the interest to not only help the toy drive, but OMSAR and the entire town."

"Wow, that sounds great. I can't wait to hear more."

"Picture this." As she sipped her coffee, Christian spread his hands like he was reading from a marquee. "Christmas Magic in Hood Hamlet."

Coffee spewed from her mouth and covered the breakfast bar.

Uh-oh. Not the reaction he expected.

She reached for a paper towel. "Please, Welton, tell me you're kidding."

"Seriously?" Leanne looked at each one of her friends sitting around the table at the brewpub that night. She'd known Sean Hughes, Jake Porter, Bill Paulson and Tim Moreno for more years than she wanted to count. She'd grown up with them. They were her climbing partners and her friends. The closet thing to family she had. But right now she couldn't believe they were buying into Welton's insane idea.

"Christmas Magic in Hood Hamlet?" she asked them. "A day long celebration with sleigh rides, sledding, caroling and a dinner with a silent auction where attendees not only have to purchase a ticket but also donate a new toy to attend?"

"The rookie's hit this one out of the park," Bill said.

The rookie had excused himself from the table to use the restroom. She wished he'd stay there.

Okay, she appreciated Welton being there to get the ladder for her this morning. The concern in his voice when he'd called her Leanne while she was hangdogging from the roof was pretty darn sweet. But this idea of his?

It had messed up her entire day. She'd even put off getting a Christmas tree in order to tell him all the reasons this wouldn't work. Nothing she'd said dampened his enthusiasm. She'd been forced to bring in reinforcements tonight. She thought her friends would convince Welton his idea would never work. Unfortunately that hadn't happened.

"This is not hitting it out of the park. More like a pop fly to the infield," she said. "We'd have to do this the weekend before Christmas. Two weeks isn't enough time to pull it off."

"It's an ambitious idea," Sean said. "But a Christmas celebration is a perfect way to entice visitors and shoppers to Hood Hamlet, increase donations to the fire station's toy drive and raise some much needed money for OMSAR."

Tim nodded. "This is a very good idea, Leanne. The snowboard shop could use some new customers."

She stared at her mug sitting on the table. A drop of condensation ran down the side of the glass. "And here I thought you guys would be the voices of reason."

"With the economy the way it is, this is reasonable. We could all use some more business," Jake said.

Okay, the brewpub wasn't as crowded as it normally was this time of year. OMSAR was funded by donations and grants. And the toy drive… "But Christmas magic?"

Simply saying the words left a bitter taste in her mouth.

"I can't think of anything better," Tim said. "The celebration could become a yearly tradition in Hood Hamlet."

The others nodded. The enthusiasm seemed contagious.

Unbelievable. Leanne took a sip of the hand-crafted root beer the brewpub made. She was outnumbered.

Welton returned to the table. He sat across from her. "Did she try to talk you out of going along with my idea?"

Jake laughed. "Yes, but she's been trying to talk us out of doing things since she met us."

"So far it hasn't work," Sean said.

"Yeah, we just end up dragging her along with us," Bill said.

"But we always give her points for trying to be the voice of reason." Tim grinned. "I can still hear Nick saying, 'Come on, LeLe, you gotta go. Who else will save our sorry butts when we get in over our heads?'"

Amusement danced in Welton's eyes. "LeLe?"

She narrowed hers. "Don't even think about it."

"I won't," he said quickly.

"Only Nick ever called her that," Jake warned good-naturedly. "And only when he was trying to convince her to do something she knew better than to do."

"Something we usually knew better than to do, too," Bill added.

Those were the days, Leanne thought with a twinge of sadness. She sipped her root beer.

"Nick?" Christian asked.

She realized he probably didn't know who they were talking about. "Nick Bishop. Paulson mentioned him in the interview with Rachel."

"I remember now," Christian said.

"Nick was my wife's brother and my best friend since kindergarten." Jake's gaze met hers. "Leanne, you know Nick would be behind this Christmas celebration a hundred and ten percent."

Darn him. She frowned. Pulling the Nick card wasn't fair. Nick had been the first boy she kissed. A secret. An experiment. A mistake. A good thing they were smart enough to realize, even as teens, they were better as friends. Nick and Jake had taught her and Paulson how to climb. When he'd married his wife, Hannah, Leanne had thrown the bachelorette party and been a bridesmaid.

"Yeah, I suppose he would," she admitted. "But it's going to take a lot of work."

"Everybody is going to want to be involved." Sean took a chip from the basket in the center of the table. "Think total community effort. Zoe will be all over this."

Jake nodded. "Carly, too."

"Rita will want to be involved," Tim said.

Leanne looked each of the three married men in the eyes. "Don't you dare put this on your wives."

"Of course not."

"Never."

"You know us better that that."

"Yeah, I do." She eyed them warily. "That's why each of you will be as involved as they are."

Bill raised his beer. "So glad I don't have a wife."

"Me, too," Welton agreed.

"You single guys aren't getting out of this, either." An idea formed in her head, a wonderful way to get back at the rookie for suggesting the event in the first place. "This is going to be a team effort. And I know exactly who should be in charge."

"You," Welton said, as if it were a done deal.

She grinned. "No. You."

He drew back. "Me?"

Her friends nodded with wicked smiles. About time they agreed with her. "Yes, you're the perfect chairperson."

Welton frowned. "Why me?"

"Because this event is your idea." She smiled. "And because if you're in charge all the single women in town will want to help you pull it off."

He looked shell-shocked.

Serves him right. Satisfaction flowed through her. She leaned back against her chair.

"You know," Sean said. "Something like this might be too big for one chairperson."

"Especially with only two weeks to plan it," Jake agreed. "I think cochairs would be better."

"Fairer," Tim said. "Someone with ties to OMSAR."

"Don't look at me," Bill said.

Sean laughed. "We know better than that, Paulson."

"Then who?" Leanne asked.

Everyone looked at her.

She stiffened. Her tummy did a little flip. "Wait a minute. This whole celebration thing is Welton's idea."

"True, but you're the brainchild behind the fire station's toy drive," Bill said.

Welton nodded, his eyes alight with mischief. "You're also a member of OMSAR. Since they'll receive the money raised from the dinner and silent auction, it makes perfect sense for you to cochair the event with me."

"This makes no sense at all." She couldn't understand why he and the others looked so pleased with themselves. "Guys, you have to know I'm the wrong person for this. I don't believe in Christmas magic."

Jake grinned wryly. "Then maybe this will help you have a change of heart."

A change of heart? That was so not going to happen.

Her gaze collided with Welton's.

He flashed her a devastating grin.

Leanne glared at him. The pretty boy better think twice about trying to make her feel good about this. She was immune to his charm. It was his fault she'd been dragged into this Christmas magic nightmare.

And she wasn't about to let him forget it.

CHAPTER FIVE

SHIFT change the next morning reminded Christian of his first day at the station. Excitement balled in his gut. Anticipation made him sit on the front of his chair around the dining table.

Cleared for full duty.

The four sweetest words the chief had said to Christian since hiring him. No more interviews. No more watching the engine head out to a call without him. He could do what he was paid to do, what he wanted to do—help people.

He couldn't wait.

"Good call on the doughnuts, Welton." One of his roommates, Riley Hansen from B shift, snagged a maple bar out of the almost-empty pink box. The other box sat in the recycle bin after its doughnuts had disappeared faster than crab legs at a buffet. "But next time bring three dozen."

Paulson set his coffee cup on the table. "Yeah, and get a couple of the sprinkle ones, too."

Christian had brought in a bag of Stumptown Coffee beans and two dozen doughnuts this morning. He appreciated his firefighter brothers' support of him and his family during and after the rescue, even though they would chide him about his experience for days, possibly weeks to come. But after a year of being treated like the family cat or the shift's glorified maid, he was used to it. A rite of passage for the crew. He wouldn't want to work anywhere else or with any other guys. Or girl.

Make that woman.

He glanced at Thomas standing at the far end of the room. She wore her hair in a tight ponytail. She leaned against the wall with a coffee cup in her hand. No doughnut in sight. Strange. She usually dug right in. Unless he'd bought the wrong type.

"Sprinkles, huh?" Christian knew he'd purchased the right coffee beans. She'd always said the popular coffee roaster in Portland was her favorite, which was why he'd picked up a bag. "I didn't think those were Thomas's style."

"They're not." Paulson's mouth quirked. "She's plain old-fashioned all the way."

"Better than being iced with nuts like you." She grinned wryly. "I mean, yours."

A looked passed between the two, a sort of unspoken understanding. As Paulson bit into his chocolate iced doughnut with nuts on top, Christian's gaze bounced between the two. He knew they'd grown up and climbed together, but he'd never noticed how close they were. Was there more to their friendship?

The officers entered the room. Each morning the off-going officer met with the incoming one to discuss the events and calls of the previous day, apparatus problems or equipment issues and any other pertinent information the new shift needed to know. After that the crews would be briefed.

The lieutenant stood. "The apparatus maintenance was completed by B shift. That leaves C shift the station maintenance."

Christian's gaze drifted to Thomas, who listened intently. The way she pursed her lips was kind of cute. She'd done the same thing at the brewpub. A habit or effort in self-control?

As the lieutenant talked about the maintenance needing to be completed today, Christian studied her. He'd guess the latter.

Thomas held her temper in check most of the time, but Christian had glimpsed the fire in her eyes last night. The dancing flames had made her look angry and sexy at the same time. Very…intriguing.

As the lieutenant sat, the chief stood. "We're implementing a new training workout. With Christmas coming up, we'll see lots of baked goods being dropped off from patients. Be prepared to sweat, people. You need to stay in shape."

Guys muttered comments under their breaths. Not Thomas. Her eyes gleamed with excitement. She loved any form of exercise. The more brutal, the better. They would be in trouble and puking their guts out if she ever decided to take the lieutenant's exam and be in charge of physical training.

"That's all I've got for you today. Don't forget about the toy drive," the chief added. "A lot of kids are counting on us. Remind your friends about the donation barrels. Thomas dropped off one at the library and another at the General Store."

This would be the perfect time to announce the upcoming Christmas celebration. Christian glanced at Thomas, hoping to catch her attention, but she didn't glance his way. He waited for her to speak up since the toy drive was her pet project. She didn't. That meant it was up to him.

He raised his hand.

"Welton," the chief said.

Thomas glared at him from across the room. The intense sparks flaring in her brown eyes would have burned him if he'd been closer. But her lips weren't pursed like last night.

She mouthed a single word. *No.*

Her reaction amused him. He grinned.

Thomas liked things a certain way. Her way. She wasn't happy when things didn't go as she expected like at the brewpub. But he hadn't expected that same anger today. He'd riled her up…again.

"Welton," the chief repeated.

Christian needed to work with Thomas if they were going to pull off the celebration. She already didn't want to do this. Antagonizing her more wouldn't help matters. He'd wait and wrangle this out in private. "There's a sale going on at the toy store at the mall, Chief."

The irritation disappeared from Thomas's eyes. Her lips pressed together forming a thin, tight line.

She needed to smile. Lighten up. Maybe a kiss would do it.

What the hell? This was the second time he'd thought about doing that. Thomas and the word kiss didn't belong in the same sentence. Especially at work.

Christian liked challenges, but Thomas would be an impossible one. She'd never go for it. He couldn't imagine her, Ms. Perfect Paramedic, forgetting about the station's taboo and messing around with a coworker. Too bad really.

"I'll pass that along to the missus," the chief said. "Anything—"

A series of tones blared over the speaker. "Rescue 1 and Engine 3 responding to a car accident on Highway 26, five miles east of town center," the female dispatcher said.

A surge of adrenaline brought him to his feet.

"Right back into the fire, Welton," Paulson said.

Christian headed out of the dining area. "Yeah."

He was up for the physical portion of responding to a call, but he hoped this was a fender bender and not something more serious. Car accidents were rarely easy calls to deal with.

By the time he reached the engine, Thomas had jumped on her bunker gear and was climbing into the rescue rig.

Always the first one to the truck.

Christian unzipped his boots and removed them. He jumped into his bunkers and slid his socked feet into the boots. He pulled up the suspenders.

Ready to go.

He climbed into the engine, taking his usual seat behind the driver, and fastened his seat belt.

The rescue rig pulled out of the station. They were usually the first responders at a scene no matter if Thomas was on duty or not. She'd set the bar high for all the medics at the station regardless of shift.

Paulson had told Christian the crew used to bet whether one of them could beat Thomas to the truck. No one ever did. The running joke was she would be first until she retired. Or if she ever got caught naked in the shower.

He wouldn't mind seeing that.

Christian took his role and responsibilities as a firefighter seriously, but he'd never seen anyone as driven as Thomas. She might be hard-nosed and a stickler for rules, but he admired how hard she worked. He had no doubt she would put the same effort into the Christmas celebration, even though she'd shown zero enthusiasm yesterday.

He was actually looking forward to working with her. Maybe she'd annoy him enough by the time the event planning was over, he would stop thinking about kissing her. He imagined her in the shower. Then again, maybe not.

O'Ryan drove to the accident. He preferred being behind the wheel. Leanne didn't mind one bit.

The rig's studded tires crunched against the snow-covered road. The siren blared. Traffic on Highway 26 moved to the right to let them pass.

Standard procedure for any call.

Too bad this didn't feel like a normal call to her.

The knot of uneasiness in Leanne's stomach matched the pressure at her temples.

Car accident on Highway 26, five miles east of town center.

She hated responding to car accidents. But this one hit a little too close to home for her…

Don't think about it.

"You up for the new workout?" she asked.

"No."

"I am." She massaged her throbbing forehead. A headache threatened to erupt. "It'll be good for all of us."

"You know what they say, Thomas, all work and no play."

"Oh, I play."

"I haven't heard about you playing with any guys in a long time." O'Ryan passed a school bus. "Still getting over that physical therapist from Hood River?"

"Long over him. Just taking a break from dating right now."

O'Ryan winked. "You could always date a firefighter."

"I know better than to get involved with one of you guys."

"Yeah, the chief wouldn't like that."

A sheriff's deputy's flashing blue-and-red lights shone in the distance.

Her throat tightened. "It's a small station in an even smaller town. Why borrow trouble?"

"I hear you on that." O'Ryan tapped the brakes of the medic rig. The studded tires bit into the layer of snow and ice. "Damn. This is a bad one."

Leanne stared out the medic rig's windshield as they approached the accident scene.

Flashing lights. Cars. People. Falling snow. Glass. Blood. A blanket covered a body on the road.

She glimpsed what might have once been a minivan. Air bags had deployed. The front was smashed all the way into the driver's seat. The side windows had shattered. The left side had buckled. She couldn't see the other side.

A few feet away rested an SUV spun at a weird angle with its front end and right side crushed. A police officer leaned over a passenger in the SUV, someone covered in red. In blood.

Images flashed through her mind like a movie on fast forward. Bursts of colors. Explosions of sounds. Tears of pain.

Hang on. They'll be here soon.

She closed her eyes. It didn't help stop the pictures or the memories.

The metallic taste of blood filled her mouth. Her stomach clenched. She wanted to throw up. Leanne clutched the arm handle until her knuckles turned white.

"Thomas."

She opened her eyes. She couldn't let anyone see how much this was affecting her.

Focus. She had a job to do, people to help, possibly lives to save. "I'll take the minivan. You take the SUV. Let me know what you have so we can see if we need more help out here."

The rig stopped.

She opened the door and jumped out. The frigid air made her suck in a sharp breath, one that hurt her lungs.

Screams and cries filled the air. A child wanted his mommy. Familiar sounds. Smells. Emotions.

Bile rose in her throat.

Focus, Thomas. Leanne grabbed equipment from the rig. People were counting on her to be able to hold herself together. She'd done it more times than she could count. She could do it again.

Hang on. They'll be here soon.

Not soon. Now.

With the trauma kit in her hands, she ran to the minivan.

The chatter over the radio told Christian this accident was more serious than the fender bender they'd responded to last week. At least one casualty.

The engine approached the scene.

Two vehicles. One minivan. One SUV. Police cars blocked traffic. A stuffed pink elephant lay on the snow-covered road.

Damn. His jaw tensed.

On the ground, Thomas performed CPR on a patient. A sheriff's deputy, Will Townsend, assisted her. At the mangled SUV, O'Ryan leaned halfway inside.

"This doesn't look good," Paulson muttered.

"Nope," Christian agreed.

"Welton," the lieutenant said through his headset. "Jaws of life."

"Got it," he said.

The engine stopped. Christian unfastened his seat belt and opened the door.

Time to get back into the game. He was ready.

After dinner that night, Christian emptied the dishwasher. He felt as if he'd worked a double shift, but still had half of his single one to go. Outside the kitchen window, an overcast sky hid the moon, but he wondered if the big, round ball of light was hanging up there somewhere. A full moon could explain the craziness of today. Since this morning's car accident, they'd barely had time to restock supplies after each call before being sent out again. The entire crew seemed wiped out, especially the medics.

The din of the television in the other room could barely be heard over O'Ryan's snores. The EMT had fallen asleep in one of the lounge chairs as soon as dinner was over. Thomas was nowhere to be seen. She'd been quiet, almost distracted, during the meal. She'd barely touched her dinner—one Christian had offered to cook in Paulson's place—before disappearing. Upstairs in the bunk room, perhaps?

Christian wouldn't blame her for calling it an early night. He understood why she might be upset. The car accident's three fatalities would have been enough for one day. But also losing a heart-attack patient on the way to the hospital, a teen with a traumatic brain injury following a sledding accident and a baby bitten by a dog didn't make for the easiest of days. The medical reports alone had to be daunting. Not that easy was part of the job description.

Paulson entered the kitchen. He made a beeline for the brownies the lieutenant's wife and kids had dropped off during dinner. He placed one on a napkin and wrapped it up.

"Midnight snack?" Christian asked.

"For Thomas," Paulson said. "She'll be hungry later."

His comment piqued Christian's curiosity. Paulson had a reputation around town with the ladies. Unless that was a smoke screen for his so-called "friendship" with Thomas.

"I haven't seen her since dinner," Christian said.

"She's up in the bunk room." Paulson wrapped another brownie in a napkin. "Calls with kids are the worst. She takes them pretty hard."

Christian nodded. He would never forget one of his first. A crying father had placed his nonbreathing two-year-old in Christian's arms. That had shaken him up for days. He'd learned fast to focus on the calls they could help and forget about the ones they couldn't. Easier said than done.

"Maybe it'll be a slow night," Christian said.

"Maybe." Paulson scribbled Thomas's name on the napkin.

Familiar tones sounded over the loudspeaker. "Rescue 1 and Engine 3 to RV fire."

"And then, maybe not," Paulson said.

Christian exited the kitchen. Before he reached the truck, Thomas had jumped into her bunkers.

Damn. He climbed into his gear. How did she get down here so fast? She looked sleep rumpled with her crooked ponytail. Dark circles ringed her eyes. Christian's stomach knotted. Upset didn't begin to describe the sadness he saw in her eyes or the uneasy expression on her face.

Leanne didn't need a brownie. She needed a hug.

He took his seat in the engine.

As the engine followed the rescue rig out of the station, Christian couldn't stop thinking about her. He wondered who would be the one hugging her when she finished her shift tomorrow morning. Some guy here at the station like Paulson or…someone else?

Christian wished it could be…him.

At one o'clock in the morning, Leanne restocked medical equipment on the rig. She needed to have the necessary supplies in case they received another call. Given the day so far, they most likely would.

A shiver inched down her spine. Not in anticipation of what might happen, but dread.

Ridiculous.

The car accident this morning was to blame for the way she felt, not the other calls. But she'd held herself together, done her duty and transported a critical patient to one of the best trauma centers in the Pacific Northwest. She hadn't had this kind of reaction in a couple of years. Maybe this would be the last time.

She knew the routine.

Never show weakness. Never admit you care. Empathy would only lead to a nervous breakdown.

As Leanne added additional IV supplies to the trauma kit, images from the car accident flashed through her mind. Not even a shower could get rid of the smells. Not that they were real. Just her imagination now.

She closed the kit and latched it. The rig was ready to go the next time a call came in. The rest of the crew had called it a night after the long day. But she wasn't ready for bed. A much needed nap after dinner had given her a second wind. Maybe she'd...

Leanne sensed a presence behind her. The familiar soap scent filled her nostrils. She wanted another sniff.

Bad idea. The guy was trouble with a capital *T*. "What do you want, Welton?"

"You're still awake."

"Wow." She didn't turn around. "They really teach amazing powers of observation at OSU."

"How do you know I went to Oregon State?"

She heard the surprise in his voice. "The Portland paper published your entire biography in the paper. Owen's, too."

He swore under his breath.

"You didn't know," she said.

"No."

The one word spoke volumes. Leanne shouldn't take the way she felt out on Welton.

She turned. The moment her gaze met his, unexpected warmth surged through her veins.

"I've tried not to pay attention to the press coverage or the comments that must have followed," he said.

Smart man. "A few details were mixed up in the articles, but that happens when you have reporters, who aren't climbers, trying to write stories."

"The comments..."

She didn't want him to worry about something out of his

control. Not that he seemed like the anxious type. "Typical rants about taxpayers having to pay for rescues, climbing Hood in the winter, the need for Mountain Locator Units. You've probably read the same comments every time something goes wrong up there."

"Yeah." His gaze grew serious. "Even if we'd had a MLU, you wouldn't have reached us any sooner because of the storm."

"Exactly. An MLU would have made no difference. You gave us what we needed to find you, but try telling that to the Monday morning quarterbacks," she said. "They always think they know best even if they wouldn't know a biner from a key ring."

Christian's easy smile crinkled the corners of his blue eyes. Those eyes hinted at a secret hidden in their depths, captivating her.

Leanne didn't want to look away. She couldn't.

Something between them had changed since the rescue. Leanne wished she knew what. Sure, she'd always found Welton attractive, but she'd never been so…aware and affected by him before.

He didn't seem to be in any hurry to break the contact, either. "It was a rough day. You okay?"

Her pulse quickened. "Why wouldn't I be okay?"

"You seemed a little uneasy, distracted at dinner. You're up now."

Her heart pounded against her ribs. Forget that he was a hottie, she didn't like that Welton could read her so well. "I've had a few things on my mind. Your dinner was good."

"I didn't see you eat much."

"You're not turning into some watch-my-every move stalker type, are you?"

He smiled. "Nope, just concerned about a fellow firefighter."

His words wrapped around her heart like a fleece blanket. Exactly what she needed right now. She really didn't like that. "Uh, thanks. But I'm fine."

"Hungry?"

Not hungry. Starving. Nodding, she lowered her gaze to his lips. Her mouth went dry.

"Paulson saved you a brownie," Welton said.

Leanne would rather have a taste of him. Uh-oh. Where had that come from? Okay, she'd been staring at his lips, but she shouldn't be thinking of Welton *that* way. Look, don't touch or taste. She nearly groaned as the sharp desire to do just that gripped her in a tight vise. "A brownie sounds good."

The words came out in a rush like water spewing from a broken fire hydrant. So unlike her. Maybe she should forget the chocolate and call it a night before she did or said something stupid.

"It's on the counter in the kitchen," he said. "Paulson wrapped it up in a napkin and wrote your name on it."

For all of Paulson's lack of maturity and womanizing ways, the guy was such a great friend. Always had been. "Thanks."

Eager to put some distance between her and Welton, Leanne walked toward the kitchen.

He fell in step next to her. "You and Paulson are close."

She wished the guy would leave her alone. "We've known each other for almost twenty-five years. He's one of my best friends."

"Close friends are hard to find."

"They are." She entered the kitchen and saw the wrapped brownie. "Especially ones who know the importance of choc-olate."

"You climb with Paulson."

"I let him climb with me."

Christian laughed.

The rich sound filled the kitchen and made her a little dizzy. He had a great laugh. Not that it mattered. She bit into her brownie.

"So are you just friends or…?"

Welton's suggestive tone made Leanne choke on the brownie. She swallowed. "Friends. Period. Why would you think—?"

"He saved you a brownie."

She pointed to another wrapped brownie on the counter. "He saved one for O'Ryan, too."

"I didn't know that."

"Why do you care anyway?" Leanne eyed him warily. "You've never seemed interested in station gossip before."

"We're going to be working together on the Christmas event," Welton said. "I thought it might be good to get to know you better. You know my dating situation. I figured fair is fair."

"I'm not dating Paulson," she admitted. "Love the guy like a brother, but that's as far as it will ever go."

"But you are dating someone…"

She raised an eyebrow. "Is this really relative to us being cochairs?"

"Do you always answer a question with a question?" Welton countered.

"I'm not dating anyone at the moment."

Even the most macho, secure guys seemed intimidated by her job, her hobbies and especially her male friends and coworkers. She took another bite of the brownie. At least she had chocolate.

"So you were dating someone," Christian prompted.

She'd really liked Blake. Thought it might go somewhere. "It was a while ago. Summer."

"What happened?"

Most of the crew, with the exception of O'Ryan and Paulson, only cared about their own love life, not hers. "You really want to know?"

"Yes."

Welton sounded genuine. He really seemed to care. She kind of liked that. "Blake was a physical therapist from Hood River. A decent guy. We had fun, but he had issues with me working on an all male twenty-four hour shift. He didn't want me spending any time with my mountain rescue friends, either." Leanne stared at her bare ring finger. The one thing she'd dreamed of was having a family of her own. But that didn't seem likely of happening anytime soon. "Blake resented my job at the station and my volunteering with OMSAR. He told me he wanted a woman who needed to be taken care of by him not one who worked in a team surrounded by other men."

"That sure isn't you."

"Those were almost his exact words." She'd heard from a mutual friend, who worked in the nearest Emergency Department, that Blake had gotten engaged to a real-estate agent. Leanne raised the brownie to her mouth. "No big loss."

She took a bite. Chocolate always made things better.

"A guy like that would never be able to make you happy," Christian said. "So tomorrow…"

She wiped her mouth with the napkin. "What about tomorrow?"

"You and me. A little Christmas magic."

Seriously? Leanne gave him a look that should have sent him scurrying back and ducking for cover. He didn't flinch. She would try another tact. "Please tell me you've never actually used that line on a woman."

His grin could charm the underpants off an avowed spinster. "You have to admit, it's a pretty good line. Might have to add that to the arsenal."

A reluctant smile tugged at her lips. The guy was something else. She had to admit he was making her feel a little better. "You have weapons?"

"WMDs, baby." Mischief gleamed in his eyes. "Want to inspect them?"

Leanne laughed. Welton was good for lightening the mood around here. She appreciated that about him. "I'll pass, but I'm sure you won't have any trouble finding someone who wants to give them a close examination."

"So tomorrow—"

"I'm hitting the backcountry." Maybe that would remove the weight pressing against the center of her chest from this morning's accident. Fresh air and snow were the perfect combination to make her forget everything else. "All that powder is calling to me."

Maybe now he'd leave her alone.

Christian rocked back on his heels. "I'd be up for making a few laps if you want some company."

Anticipation shot through her. She hadn't expected him to want to go. "Do you have the gear?"

"If by gear you mean skins, shovel, probe and beacon. Yeah, I've got them." He set his chin. "I know how to use them, too."

Leanne really shouldn't. But she had offered to go skiing with him when they'd been at the Sno-Cat. Maybe she should get it over with tomorrow. She wanted things to go back to the way they'd been before the rescue when she was satisfied looking at Welton, but not wanting to touch him. Kiss him.

His charming smile spread all the way to his eyes and took her breath away. "Wondering if you can keep up with me?"

"No." Welton might be hot stuff down here, but up on the mountain was another story. That was one place she could hold her own against any guy without even trying. "Wondering if you can keep up with me."

"I'm always up for a challenge," he said. "In fact, we can put a little wager on it."

She raised brow. "Such as."

"Dinner."

Her heart leaped. Oh, no. Wrong reaction. "I hope you don't mean a date, Welton."

"I know better than that, Thomas. I meant the loser has to take the winner's turn cooking dinner at the station."

Leanne should have known he wasn't talking about a date. She ignored the twinge of disappointment. Welton was a coworker. Nothing else. As long as she kept remembering that, she would be fine. And this outing was going to be good. Fun. Exactly what she needed. "You're on."

"You're going down, Thomas."

She fought the urge to laugh at her impending victory. Welton would be begging for oxygen by the time she finished with him. She would stop thinking about him as anything more than a showboating rookie who she had rightly put back in his place. Yeah, this was exactly what she needed to put the rescue and all these weird feelings behind her. "We'll see about that."

CHAPTER SIX

A PERFECT day for backcountry skiing on the northeast side of Mount Hood. The sun shone bright. No goggles, only sunglasses required. A breeze blew over the snow and through the trees. The temperature was comfortable.

Christian wore a thermal top over his ski pants. He'd shoved his jacket in his backpack before leaving the parking lot. The uphill climb would make him sweat if he wore too much. Layering clothes was key to comfort out here.

The trail from the Cooper Spur Ski Area was well traveled. With skins on the bottom of his skis to grip the snow, Christian led the way following the path of skiers and climbers who'd come before him that morning.

He glanced back at Thomas.

Two braids dangled from beneath the brim of her wool beanie. She also wore a thermal top that stretched across her chest. Her breasts bounced as she moved.

His smiled widened. A nice view. Too bad he couldn't skin backward. "Thanks for letting me tag along."

Sunglasses hid her eyes, but nothing could disguise the huge grin on her face. She looked like he felt. Carefree and loving life. "It's more fun to have company out here."

"Do you ski here a lot?"

"It depends on the weather and conditions. I try to get in as many turns in a year as I can," she explained. "There are lots of places to ski around here."

No kidding. Christian faced forward and continued up. Two

hours ago he'd been getting off his shift at the fire station. Now he was skinning his way toward the Tilly Jane Cabin with Thomas. There was nowhere else he'd rather be right now. "I want to try them all."

A party of three skied down through the charred toothpicks that used to be trees until the Gnarl Ridge fire ravaged the area in 2008. The fire came close to taking out both the cabin and the historic Cloud Cap Inn, but was contained in time.

Snow flew from the tips of the men's skis. Some pockets of powder seemed deeper than others. The descent looked a little tricky with narrow passages between trees, lots of turns and steep, uneven trails, but still fun.

The three men whooped and hollered. Two waved in Christian's direction. He didn't recognize them and glanced back at Thomas. "Know them?"

"Yes."

Not enough information. "OMSAR."

"No."

His mouth twisted in frustration. Most women wanted Christian to ask questions about their lives. Once they started talking, they didn't stop. Not Thomas.

Most females found him attractive. A fun time. A catch.

The fact Thomas acted as if he had an infectious disease intrigued him as much as it annoyed him.

A dog barked. Around the Pacific Northwest animals frequented the trails right alongside their owners.

Christian looked toward the burnt trees. A black lab bounded through the snow, practically riding on the tails of his owners' skis.

Leanne laughed. "Now that's a ski dog."

"I wonder how he'd do on a lift."

"Mount Bachelor's K-9 Avalanche Dogs ride the lifts with their handlers." She watched the pair descend and disappear in the trees. "You'd be surprised how well dogs do. Often better than people."

Some people had problems with chairlifts. The station had

responded to calls at local ski areas. A few situations defied logic. She was probably right about dogs doing better.

Thomas usually was right. He, along with the rest of the crew, had finally resigned themselves to the fact. But one of these days she'd be wrong about something. Maybe that something would be him. Christian grinned at the thought.

The Tilly Jane Cabin came into view. Outdoor enthusiasts made the most of the A-frame structure with glass windows, a woodstove and a fireplace. A local group kept the building maintained. Overnight stays were available in the sleeping loft via a reservation system, but anyone could stop in during the day to warm up and use one of the picnic tables inside. Nothing fancy, but a good place to get out of the cold, relax and eat.

Outside the cabin, he removed his skis. "I brought hot chocolate."

"One of my favorite things." Leanne stepped out of her bindings. "I've got blueberry scones."

They chatted about climbing and ate quickly.

Fifteen minutes later with skis on, they set out again. The snowfall from yesterday had covered the previous ski tracks heading up the mountain. That would mean fresh powder runs on the way down, but breaking trail on the way up. They wouldn't have a path to follow as on their way to the cabin, but would have to make their own. That meant more work.

"I'll go first," Leanne offered.

Christian let her pass him. "We can switch off."

"Sure."

She skinned up toward the Stone Hut, another shelter like the cabin built in the 1930s for people using the Timberline Trail. After they reached the hut, they would see what the conditions were like and decide whether to continue on up to Tie-in Rock.

He followed, not minding one bit about being behind her. He enjoyed this view of her backside almost as much as he had her front.

Right away Christian knew this wasn't going to be a leisurely trek up the mountain. Thomas's skinning was more like sprinting. They gained elevation fast. He felt every vertical foot. Worse, they were still below the tree line.

A couple days in a snow cave shouldn't affect him this much. But he struggled to keep up with Thomas as she skinned higher.

The climb didn't seem to bother Leanne at all. She chatted about the Civilian Conservation Corps without sounding the slightest bit winded or tired. But as she explained how the CCC had built the Tilly Jane Cabin and several of the stone huts around Mount Hood, Christian's lungs hurt.

Was Thomas some kind of mutant? A real-life Amazon? Or a robot?

No, a robot's butt wouldn't look that nice. When she wore tank tops around the station her skin looked really soft, too. Thomas must be human, but he didn't understand why she hadn't slowed her pace up the mountain.

Maybe she wanted to win the cooking dinner bet. Maybe she wanted to show off. Maybe she wanted to show him that he wasn't as excellent a skier, athlete, insert-another-noun-here as he thought he was. Probably the last one.

"Is the pace okay?" she yelled back.

No. But he wasn't about to admit that. He could hold his own. "Fine."

Rays of light sparkled off the foot of fresh powder covering the morning. A pretty setting, but he needed to focus on moving higher.

Christian forced himself forward. One step. And another.

He couldn't breathe. Okay, he could. Or he'd be flat on his back unconscious. He just couldn't breathe very well.

Damn. If Thomas saw him like this, she wouldn't slow down. She'd turn around.

No way. Christian didn't want to be the reason they didn't make it to Tie-in Rock. He sure wasn't going to concede their bet, either.

Time to remedy the situation. Or at least hide it.

He breathed through his nose and exhaled through his

mouth. It didn't help. He tried the other way around. Still nothing.

His lungs burned like a three-alarm fire.

The distance between him and Thomas increased. She skinned uphill as if a pack of wolves chased after her. An exhausting pace, one that left him gasping for breath. But she looked like poetry in motion, her skis and her poles in perfect coordination.

Christian wanted to know her secret.

She glanced back. "Such a gorgeous day."

"Uh-huh." He couldn't talk with his breathing so ragged.

Facing forward, she broke trail as if she were walking across wet sand, not twelve inches of new snow.

The woman amazed him. Christian thought he was in shape. Not even close when it came to Thomas. She had the lungs of a world-class athlete. The legs, too. She would easily lap him if they decided to do more than one run today.

Christian winced at his words of challenge from last night. So much for trying to impress her. All he'd done was prove he was an idiot, just as Owen had said. And she'd known it as soon as Christian opened his mouth.

A few minutes later, Thomas stopped. She removed her sunglasses.

It took him longer than he liked to catch up. His heart beat like a snare drum roll.

"Let's take a break," she said.

His ego wanted him to say he didn't want one, didn't need one. They had a bet riding on today. Appearing weak wouldn't get it done. But self-preservation made him nod. A little rest and maybe he'd be good to go.

Who was he kidding? Christian was still going to lose.

Thomas shrugged off her backpack. She pulled out a water bottle, thermos and her puffy jacket. She put on her coat and sat on her pack.

All he wanted to do was sit, but he removed his pack and

took out his jacket. He sat on top of his backpack and took off his sunglasses.

She took a sip of water then passed the bottle to him. "It's going to get cold fast if we're not moving."

Christian knew that. He put on his jacket.

"I've got tea," she said.

He should have added a bottle of oxygen to his first aid kit. "Thanks."

"The breeze is stronger up here. The snow will be wind-blown near Tie-in Rock. It might be iffy around the Stone Hut, too. We might not want to go much higher."

Relief washed over him. They wouldn't be going all the way up. He hated being a wimp, but right now all he wanted to do was slow down and breathe. He drew in much needed air and willed his heart rate to slow.

She dug in the snow with her gloved hand. The casualness of the gesture made him wonder if she was even aware of doing it. She fit so well out here.

Guilt coated the inside of his mouth. She might be disappointed about not skinning all the way to Tie-in Rock. "If you want to go up and check conditions—"

"Not today."

Christian should leave it, but he couldn't. "Earlier, you sounded excited to go up."

"I changed my mind."

"But—"

Her gaze met his in unspoken understanding. Not pity, but empathy. The tender expression in her eyes reached all the way to his heart.

She was giving him a way out without having to admit he was tired, winded and not in as good of shape as her. A way to save face even though they both knew he wasn't up to it. His respect for her increased exponentially. His admiration, too. But she didn't need to spare his ego.

"You don't have to pretend," he said.

She pulled out a plastic baggie full of trail mix. "What are you talking about?"

"I'm man enough to admit when I'm beat."

Her eyes widened. "You're conceding?"

"Only the ascent." He wanted to take a shot at beating her down. "I'm man enough to let you lead on your own turf."

"No one's ever said that to me." She sounded surprised, pleased.

"I'm not just any guy."

"You sure aren't."

Her words made Christian sit taller. "Wait until we're on my turf. Smith Rock. It'll be a different story then."

"I'm looking forward to it." Her voice held a hint of anticipation. She held up the bag of trail mix. "Hungry?"

"Yes." Thomas handed him the bag, and he took some. "Thanks."

She leaned back and gazed off into the distance. "I love it out here."

Christian followed her line of sight—a beautiful view of the Eliot Glacier. Snow, rock and blue sky greeted him. "Wow."

"*Wow* sums it up perfectly. I couldn't imagine living anywhere else in the world. I wouldn't want to."

He looked back at her. His breath caught in his throat.

Joy radiated from Thomas.

Beautiful. Serene. Two adjectives he'd never used with Thomas before fit her now.

Thomas inhaled deeply. She leaned her head back farther. Her jacket opened. Her thermal shirt tightened across her breasts.

Hot. Christian's pulse skyrocketed. If not for every muscle aching and his gasping for breath…

No, he still couldn't make a move on her. But he could enjoy the view. Christian shouldn't, but he sneaked a peek for a few extra—

"Up here," she said. "I feel as if I'm that much closer to heaven."

Jerk. He was leering at her breasts like a randy teenager while she was opening up to him. Christian wanted to redeem himself. "A good feeling."

She glanced his way. Her gaze locked on his.

His heartbeat stumbled.

"The best," she said.

Thomas removed another plastic baggie from her backpack. She broke off a small piece of a half-eaten scone and held it in the air.

A gray bird with a white forehead appeared out of nowhere and landed on Thomas's hand. The small beak picked at the scone. "Gray jays love people food."

"I've heard about them, but never seen one up close." He studied the bird. "So tame eating right off your palm like that."

"They don't migrate." She added more food to her hand. The bird helped itself. "They hoard food so they have enough to last through winter."

"Or steal yours."

Her gaze softened, making his heart beat in double time. She was attractive, sexy, dangerous. He bet she would want to call the shots when it came to romance. She might even be too much for him to handle. He definitely couldn't keep up with her out here, but she was still oh-so-tempting.

"Not stealing," she said. "I'm giving the food to him."

"It could be a her."

"They do look alike." She handed him the baggie. "Try it."

"I don't want to take your little bird away."

She smiled. "Gray jays travel in pairs."

"Everyone needs a wingman," he teased.

"Gray jays are monogamous."

He made a face.

"Let me guess," she said. "You hate that word as much as you dislike relationship, girlfriend, commitment."

"Yeah, but how do you know that?"

"Jake, Sean and Bill." She watched the bird eat. "A few other guys in the unit. And the station."

"You have a lot of guy friends."

"Occupational hazard in my line of work, but I have a few girlfriends."

Christian remembered what she'd said at her town house. "Zoe Hughes."

Leanne placed a little of the scone on her hand. "Carly Porter and Hannah Willingham, too."

Two more gray jays flew down from the trees and landed on his arm. "Monogamous, huh? I'd like to know how the third one gets to come along. Never knew birds could be so kinky."

She released a drawn out sigh. "Get you're mind out of the gutter, Welton. Sometimes a younger bird stays with the parents or an older couple for a while. Nothing kinky."

"Sticking around your family is boring." He put out more of the scone for the birds. "Kinky is lots more fun."

"Family is wonderful."

"Not when they want you to leave the place you love and move home."

Christian's shoulder muscle stiffened. He'd said more than he intended.

"Your family doesn't like you living in Hood Hamlet."

It wasn't a question. But he didn't want to leave her hanging the way she'd left him. "No, but I love it here. I'm not about to be pressured into moving back to the Willamette Valley, no matter what they offer me."

"But they're family." The passion in her voice surprised him. Her eyes deepened to that sexy dark chocolate color. She touched his arm. "Family is so important, Welton. You have no idea how lucky you are to have people who love you so much. Find a way to work things out. Compromise."

Christian had never seen Thomas act this way. He liked her hand on his, the pressure firm but comfortable. "My grandfather doesn't know the meaning of the word compromise. He'll do whatever it takes to force me to do what he wants."

Her fingers squeezed his hand. "Force you?"

"Bribe me is probably a better way to describe it, but I've

held my ground," Christian said. "When I was younger I needed to figure out what I wanted out of life. He didn't want me to leave, even though I needed to figure out what was important to me and what wasn't."

She pulled her hand away. "What did you do?"

"I packed my car and left home for eighteen months."

Her mouth gaped. "A year and a half? What did you do for all that time?"

"Rock climbed," he said. "All over the United States. Tuolumne, Eastern Sierras, Tetons, Boulder Canyon, City of Rocks, Devil's Tower, Vedauwoo. The list goes on. I lived like a dirtbag. Slept in my car or tent. Washed in bathrooms. Avoided private investigators my grandfather sent after me. Had the time of my life."

"Why'd you stop?" she asked.

"Got tired of living like a dirtbag. The investigator caught up with me. I missed my family. I realized they were important to me, after all."

But he hadn't been important to one of them, to his ex-fiancée. Christian didn't want to think about her and what she'd wanted him to do.

Thomas's gaze never left his. "It had to be better when you went home."

He nodded. "Until I became a volunteer firefighter. I was working at the winery, too, but that wasn't enough for my grandfather. He offered me one hundred thousand dollars. Handed me a check with my name on it. A year's salary up-front. I just had to quit firefighting and only work at the winery."

"That's a lot of money to turn down."

Christian stared off into the distant. "I liked working at the winery, but I loved firefighting. I wanted to do both. I knew I could do both. No way could I accept the money. My dad always took whatever carrot my grandfather dangled. Giving into that pressure cost my dad his marriage to my mother and his life. He died of a heart attack from all the stress when he was in his forties."

"I'm so sorry, Christian."

"Thanks," he said. "My dad made his own choices, and I'm making mine. If I choose to do something, it's going to be on my terms, not someone else's."

"Makes sense," she agreed. "Have you explained this to your family?"

"I've tried, but…"

"Maybe it's time to try again," she encouraged.

Christian stared at the three birds—a family. He hadn't felt like part of his family until the rescue on the mountain. "Maybe I should. The rescue seems to have changed things. My grandfather wants the family Christmas celebration to be in Hood Hamlet even though he's never visited me before. He's rented a huge house for all of us."

"That sounds wonderful."

"We'll see. Nothing has ever come without strings attached," he admitted. "We might end up having a very blue Christmas."

"I'm sure it'll be great." She sounded sincere and a bit wistful. "Families should be together on Christmas."

"Is your family around here?" he asked.

"Not too far away location wise, but in a completely different place."

"I know that feeling."

Her eyes clouded, but she didn't say anything.

The three birds flew away.

She watched them go then placed her baggie inside her pack. "Ready to ski?"

"I could skin up a little farther."

Leanne eyed him cautiously.

"If I'm the one breaking trail." And setting the pace. Otherwise, he'd be doomed.

"Go for it." She winked. "I want to see what you've got."

Her playfulness pleased him. All of her did. Being with

Thomas out here was cool even though she'd kicked his butt skinning. "Great."

"Yeah." Her grin seemed a constant up here on the mountain. "I'll have more energy to beat you down."

Her eyes sparkled and matched the beaming smile on her face. A fresh pink colored her cheeks. He'd never seen a woman so full of life, healthy and vibrant.

Christian stared at her mouth. He wanted to know what her lips tasted like. "I knew there had to be a catch."

"There's always a catch, Welton. Sometimes you get lucky and other times you don't."

He flashed his most devilishly charming smile. Most women appreciated it. Maybe Thomas would. "I like getting lucky."

"Feeling lucky today?"

Her flirty tone sent his temperature up ten degrees. "Yeah."

She brushed the crumbs off her lap and stood. "Then let's get going. I have a bet to win."

"I still have a chance."

Not with skiing, but with her.

She gave him the once-over. "I never knew you were such an optimist, Welton."

"I always knew you were so cynical," he teased.

Amusement twinkled in her eyes. "Try it, you might like it."

He'd like to try something, all right. He was pretty sure he'd like it. Her.

She drank a sip of water. The tip of her tongue darted out and ran over her lips.

Christian liked flirting with her. He liked being with her. The more he learned about Thomas, the more intrigued he became. His usual tricks weren't going to work with someone like her. She was so confident, so comfortable with men.

A challenge, yes. But not as impossible a one as Christian had first believed. He saw signs that he was cracking that hard shell of hers. She came out skiing. She flirted. He was finally getting to her. He wasn't about to give up now.

* * *

With a potent mix of excitement and adrenaline pounding through her veins, Leanne skied through the trees and the knee-deep powder. The one good thing to come from the Gnarl Ridge fire was additional ski terrain. She made the most of it today.

With Welton.

Watching him get winded on the ascent and trying to pretend as though nothing was wrong made her want to laugh. But he'd impressed her by stopping the charade and admitting defeat. She respected that. Not many men were as sure of themselves as he was.

She would love spending more time with him. He was easy to talk with, easy to hang with and easy on the eyes. He was probably easy when it came to other things.

Nope. Better not let her lonely mind to go there with the handsome firefighter. For all she knew, he might not be ready to settle in Hood Hamlet. He had things to work out with his family. He could decide to take off on another extended road trip to figure out what was important in his life now.

Leanne stopped. The edges of her skis sent snow flying into the air. She turned uphill to watch Welton ski.

Pretty impressive. She had to give him credit. Even after she'd lapped him doing extra runs—two in her case—he hadn't cursed, shot her dagger-worthy stares or puked. Definitely a different kind of guy.

Welton stopped next to her, spraying her with powder. "You're one badass, Thomas. I can't believe you lapped me and still beat me down another time."

"You sure know how to sweet-talk a lady."

"You're no lady. Not the way you just booked down the mountain. Not to mention up it."

"I'll take that as a compliment."

"Go right ahead. It is one."

That meant a lot to her. "I'm up for one more run."

Christian stared at her in disbelief. Shock, really.

She tried not to laugh. "But we can call it a day."

"You're a total ringer." He sounded amused, not upset. "You wore me out on purpose."

"Guilty as charged," she admitted. "But you deserved it for being so cocky and arrogant."

He flashed her a lopsided smile. "What if I was only trying to impress you?"

Was he serious? That would be so sweet. No, he had to be joking. "Yeah, right."

Christian didn't say anything. But that didn't mean he hadn't been teasing her.

"You did better than I thought you would. Better than a lot of guys have in the past," she admitted. "And that's a compliment, in case you were wondering."

"I'll take it." He drank water. "Can anybody keep up with you?"

"Sean Hughes. Well, before his accident last Thanksgiving, but he's getting back to where he used to be," she said. "But it's not as if I always try to ski people into the ground."

"So the bet—"

"I really like your Chicken Marsala."

Welton laughed. "I never stood a chance."

"There's always a chance," she said. "Do you want to go double or nothing?"

His smile crinkled the corners of his eyes and made Leanne's heart want to sigh. "I may be younger than you, Thomas. But I'm not stupid. No sucker bets for me anymore."

"You pick up quick, Welton."

Wicked laughter lit his eyes. "You should see what else I can pick up."

"I can imagine."

"I'd be happy to show you for real…"

The invitation hung in the air. Joking again or flirting this time? Maybe a combination?

Temptation drew her closer to him. She forced her legs to stop moving.

Silly. This was Welton. He knew better. So did she. He had to be joking. Just like at the station. Yet a part of her wished…

No, that was loneliness talking. Leanne couldn't cross that line with Welton. She couldn't take that chance even if he made her feel like…a woman. So not good. All she'd ever wanted was to fit in. She'd done that in spades both at the fire station and with OMSAR. She didn't need Welton—okay, her attraction to him—to mess that up for her.

Today had been fun. Much better than skiing solo. She enjoyed his company. But being anything other than skiing or climbing partners didn't make sense. They were at different places. Not so much age-wise, but in life. Welton liked playing the field. When she started dating again, she wanted to find Mr. Right. Best not to get too attached to him. Too close.

Leanne raised her chin. "Thanks, but I'll pass. Call Rachel or Alexa. I'm sure one of them would be happy to oblige. You've still got a few days until the breakup deadline."

Welton laughed. Definitely joking. Good.

Disappointment squeezed her chest. She adjusted her grip on her poles.

Confusion knotted Leanne's stomach. Her reaction made no sense. She wasn't looking for fun or a fling. She wanted forever.

No matter how handsome or charming or entertaining, Welton wasn't a forever kind of guy. Leanne gave him a long, hard look. Not even close.

CHAPTER SEVEN

THREE days later, Leanne stood outside Mr. Freeman's General Store on Main Street. She'd come straight from her shift. Only a few skiers, snowboarders and people heading to their jobs were out, but she noticed a change in Hood Hamlet.

Excitement buzzed in the air. So did optimism. Possibility. Hope. It was all due to one person. Welton.

She stared at the flyer she'd hung in the window.

Leanne had to laugh. She'd been wrong. Not about Christmas magic. That didn't exist. But she'd been wrong about the celebration he'd proposed.

Believe it or not, his pipe dream was becoming a reality.

The adage many hands made light work had never been truer. Adults and children, merchants and stay-at-home moms were helping to make the event happen. The downturn in the economy had hurt all of them. Now they saw a chance to change things, if they worked together.

The community effort warmed her heart.

Leanne loved Hood Hamlet. She had since the first time she visited her grandparents when she was a little girl, but seeing everyone work on the celebration made the small town feel that much more special.

Amid the snow-covered street and icicles hanging from the buildings, the sounds and sights of Christmas increased by the day. White lights and garland were a Hood Hamlet tradition, but not the lighted figurines and festive trees that had been added. The charming window displays in storefronts were new, too.

So much work. So much effort. So much love for this town and each other. She hugged the stack of flyers in her hands against her chest, careful not to wrinkle them.

Footsteps crunched on the sidewalk. Chains on tourists' cars rattled against the snow-covered road. "It's Beginning to Look a Lot Like Christmas" played from a speaker outside Muffy Steven's coffee shop. The sound of someone whistling along with the tune carried on the cold air.

Recognition blasted through her. Welton whistled at the station, too. Leanne glanced left. A family of five with a dog barreled down the street. The Norwegian elkhound pulled against the leash. She looked right, past two snowboarders.

There he was.

Taller than the others, Welton strode in her direction. He wore a striped beanie on his head. He'd changed out of the station's navy colored uniform into jeans, a blue jacket and winter boots.

His gaze met hers.

Leanne's pulse kicked up a notch. The casual style of clothing looked so great on him, almost as if he'd stepped off the pages of an outdoor magazine spread. But his killer smile made her breath catch in her throat.

Wowza. She liked seeing his smile directed straight at her. Liked it a lot. Leanne swallowed. Probably too much.

He stopped in front of her. Amusement gleamed in his eyes. "Didn't we just spend the night together?"

Heat rose up her neck. Had her face just given her away? "You, me and seven others."

"With all this time we're spending together, people are going to talk."

"It's the fifth day in row."

His gaze sharpened with interest. "You've been counting."

Uh-oh. Leanne liked being with him, but she didn't want him to get the wrong idea. "I'm only counting so I'll know when I can go back to doing what I want on my days off."

"Ski."

"And climb." Her words sounded lame. "I still haven't decorated my Christmas tree yet."

"Eight more days. That's all we have left."

She thought he liked working and spending time with her. The fact he didn't bristled. "You've been counting, too."

He glanced across the street at a family of skiers loading their gear into a minivan. "Not for the same reason as you."

What did he mean by that?

"Too bad we're not skiing this morning," he continued.

Leanne would rather be skiing with him today. Not him specifically, she corrected. Any one of her ski partners.

She straightened. The top of her head came close to the tip of his nose. Welton redefined the expression tall, dark and handsome. "Well, your event isn't going to happen without some work. You had to realize that would mean our days off."

A sheepish expression crossed his face. "I didn't really think that part through."

She laughed. "Figured as much."

He motioned to the store window. "So that's the flyer."

"Tim Moreno had them for me at the snowboard shop. Mr. Freeman waved me down to get his." She read the colorful flyer hanging on the front window of the store. "Come celebrate Christmas Magic in Hood Hamlet with a day of small town holiday fun and old-fashioned good cheer."

"Zoe did an amazing job designing it," Welton said. "I like the photograph of Main Street she used. Is it one of yours?"

Leanne was pleased he remembered her photography. "I took the picture at the tree lighting ceremony the day after Thanksgiving. The fresh snow, white lights and giant decorated Douglas fir screamed Christmastime to me."

He cocked an eyebrow. "You really aren't a Grinch except when it comes to…"

"Let's leave Christmas magic out of this, 'kay?" She handed him half the stack of papers. "We need to get these passed out."

He waved his flyers. "The list of activities has grown."

"More people stepped up after the meeting. Carly asked if we minded. I told her to do what she felt would be best for Hood Hamlet. That's what she did."

"Caroling, concerts, dogsled rides, horse drawn sleigh rides, a snowboarding demo, a snow-sculpture contest."

Leanne nodded. "Don't forget the craft bazaar, cookie decorating, card making, beer and wine tasting and the dinner and silent auction to benefit Hood Hamlet Fire and Rescue's Christmas Toy Drive and OMSAR."

"Not bad with only a few days planning."

"Not bad at all," she agreed. "People might show up."

Christian grinned wryly. "Admit it. You're impressed."

Grudging respect grew, too. "I…am."

"Knew it."

She hoped that was all he knew. Her attraction intensified each time she saw him. Better get away from him now. "You canvas that side of the street. I'll do this one."

Leanne took two steps toward Wickett's Pharmacy that served the best chocolate malts at an old-fashioned soda counter.

Welton touched her shoulder. "Wait."

She stopped, conscious of his hand on her even though she wore a camisole, a turtleneck, a fleece pullover and a soft-shell jacket. His light touch made her feel tingly. "What?"

"What's the rush? We have all day. Let's grab a cup of coffee. Do this together." He lowered his arm to his side. "I want to discuss a few things about the dinner."

Tempting, but she couldn't give in to it. She had to fight her attraction. "We have a lot to accomplish today. The flyers need to be taken to all the surrounding towns, too. And I have plans this afternoon."

"A date."

The guy needed to stop jumping to conclusions. "Babysitting."

His brows furrowed. "Babysitting?"

"Watching other people's children."

"I know what babysitting is." Christian sounded annoyed. Good. That was how he made her feel. "Whose kids?"

Austin and Kendall were biologically Nick's kids, but Garrett had adopted them. "Hannah and Garrett Willingham's."

"Okay," Christian said after a long moment. "Let's split up so we can get the flyers passed out faster. Call Hannah when you can and ask if she minds if I come over to babysit with you."

Leanne laughed. "Yeah, right."

But Christian wasn't smiling.

"Come on." Perplexed, she stared. "You can't be serious."

His eyes darkened to a midnight-blue. "Why not?"

"You don't look like the babysitting type."

"There's a babysitter profile?"

"Mary Poppins. Nanny McPhee."

He made a face. "We need to talk about the dinner. It's important."

"Yes, but—"

"I've watched kids before."

"What kids?"

"My niece." He sounded offended she'd question him. "My cousins have kids, too."

Okay, the guy was an adult, but she'd seen Paulson around kids. She gave Welton a dubious look.

"Kids like me. Ask Owen. Not that you need to call him or anything." A vein throbbed at Christian's jaw. "After the kids go to bed, you and I can work on the event."

"I don't know."

"Only eight more days to go. The longer we procrastinate—"

"I'm not procrastinating," she interrupted. "It's all happening so quickly."

"Quick is good."

"If you're climbing light and fast, yes," she said. "But if not, it's better to take your time and think things through carefully."

"There's not time for that."

Unfortunately, she knew he was right. That made this… harder.

"Ask Hannah," he said.

The papers in Leanne's hands crinkled. She loosened her grip on them. "The kids will expect you to play with them."

"Call her."

He sounded earnest, but… "Don't say I didn't warn you."

"I stand duly warned," he said. "It'll be fun."

Maybe for him. Not for her.

She was having too many odd and inappropriate thoughts involving Welton. Playing house with the hot firefighter was a recipe for disaster. One she couldn't afford. Time to take charge of the situation and stop spending so much time with him. The solution didn't appeal to her, but she didn't have a choice. She had to put an end to this now.

"You know, I'm sure you've got lots to do, Welton. Women-to-woo. Hearts to break before your second Monday in December deadline." She moistened her dry lips. "Forget about being cochair on the event. You've kicked it off. Turned it into reality. That's enough. I'll take care of the rest myself."

His eyes darkened, narrowed. "You're already in charge of the toy drive."

"I don't mind." For her self-preservation, she needed to convince him this was the best, the only. "So many of the jobs have been delegated already."

He studied her.

"Really," she said, in case he had any doubts.

Christian was thinking about it. She could tell. This was going to work.

"Sorry, Thomas," he said finally. "I can't dump all this on you in addition to the toy drive. That wouldn't be fair."

"Fair?" Her voice rose. She lowered it. "I've seen you play Ultimate Frisbee and darts. Fair isn't part of your vocabulary."

"Those things involve winning. I don't like to lose. But this is different. We're going to be cochairs and I'm babysitting with you, too."

The sincerity in his voice threw her for a loop.

Maybe he wanted to work with her, spend time with her.

Her pulse skittered. She was flattered. Interested. What was she going to do?

"After you talk to Hannah, text me her address and the time you want me there," he continued.

Leanne wanted to know what was going on. "Is there any other reason you're going to so much trouble?"

"What do you mean?" he asked.

"Ever since the mountain rescue, you've been acting different. Not that you weren't nice before, but you've been going out of your way for the toy drive and OMSAR."

And me.

He shifted his weight. "You and OMSAR did something nice for me. I'm returning the favor."

Irritation revved. "I told you that isn't necessary."

"It is to me."

Leanne ignored the unexpected twinge of disappointment. Pathetic.

She was one of the guys in his eyes. That was the way Leanne wanted it to be, but...

Being one of the guys all the time was getting really old. For the first time, she wished she knew how she could change that. Especially with...Welton.

That afternoon, Christian parked behind Thomas's car in the Willinghams' driveway. White icicle lights hung from the roof of the log cabin. A snowman wearing a rainbow-striped scarf stood in the front yard. A lone electric candle sat on a windowpane, flickering as if it were a real flame. Light glowed from the other windows. With the tall fir trees surrounding the cabin, the scene looked like something from a Christmas card.

Quaint. Homey. Inviting. He liked it.

Christian exited the truck. His boots sunk into the snow as he made his way toward the porch.

Babysitting gave him the perfect excuse not to see Alexa or Rachel tonight. He really needed to tell them it was over. At least until after Christmas. But he would probably find someone else to go out with after that.

Too bad it couldn't be Thomas, but she wanted nothing to do with him that way. She'd laughed off his asking her out when they were skiing. She'd thought he was joking, but he'd been serious. Not that he blamed her. The fire station romance taboo complicated things.

Still he preferred working with her on the Christmas celebration than going out with either of the other women. Thomas acted so serious, yet she was quick with a smile or a laugh. Genuine ones. Not fake ones to appear more interested in him. She was more comfortable to be around, didn't probe into his feelings or make him feel as if she wanted…more. She wanted nothing from him. That was so different than most everyone else in his life.

Christian climbed the porch steps.

A green wreath with a red velvet bow hung from a brass holder on the front door. The same wreath Thomas had on her door. Someone's kid must sell them.

He stood on the landing.

The sharp scent of pine filled the air. He inhaled. The smell of Christmas. Well, Christmas in Hood Hamlet.

At the winery, some holidays were less traditional than others. The year before last everything had smelled like eucalyptus around the house, even the tree. The Norman Rockwell and Thomas Kincaid versions of Christmas complete with evergreens, holly and snow appealed to Christian more than whatever current decorating trend happened to be hot. At least the family decorated, even if everything had been handpicked ahead of time by an interior designer.

He knocked on the door.

A stampede of feet sounded from inside the house. Someone yelled. Another giggled.

The door swung open. Two kids greeted him with wide grins. One was a girl around eleven or twelve. The other a boy, maybe nine or ten.

"We've been waiting for you. Leanne saw your truck out the window and told us we could open the door." The girl opened the door wider. "Come in."

"Thanks." Christian entered and closed the door behind him. Heat from the fireplace blanketed him. So did the smell of chocolate baking. He extended his arm toward her. "I'm Christian."

The girl shook his hand. "I'm Kendall."

"I'm Austin." The boy also shook Christian's hand. "You had to be rescued off the mountain."

Out of the cold and into the fire. The kid had no idea how that statement made Christian feel. No matter where he went in town someone brought it up. Maybe if the event were successful, everyone would forget what happened up on the mountain. He shrugged off his jacket and hung it on a rack by the door. "Yes. OMSAR rescued me and my cousin."

Kendall beamed. "OMSAR rocks."

"They do," Christian agreed.

Austin studied him. "It's good what happened."

The kid was the first one who had said what happened was good. "You think so, dude?"

He nodded. "Better to be rescued than be dead."

That was one way to look at it. "I'm very happy to be alive."

"Our daddy was a member of OMSAR, but he died climbing the Reid Headwall," Kendall said. "It was an accident."

Nick Bishop. Christian should have put two and two together before this. "Accidents happen sometimes."

Both kids nodded. They stared at him as if they expected him to do a magic trick or something.

"Where's Leanne?" he asked.

Austin scrunched his face. "She's upstairs changing Tyler's poopy diaper."

"So you're a firefighter like Bill and Leanne," Kendall said.

"Yes, I am."

Kendall studied Christian as if he were a science experiment. "Bill's not married. Are you?"

"Nope."

"Do you date as many girls as him?" Austin asked.

"Not quite as many." But pretty darn close.

"Good." The boy sounded relieved. "Sammy Ross says if you kiss too many girls you'll wind up with some horrible disease."

Christian stifled a laugh. His gaze bounced between the two kids who waited expectedly for a response. What could he say? He wasn't versed in having a conversation about the birds and the bees with preteens. "I, uh—"

"Sammy Ross has three older sisters," Austin added sagely.

"That explains it," Christian said. "I have an older sister, too."

"Do you want to get married?" Kendall asked.

Christian had been imagining playing a couple of games of Twister with a certain female paramedic and OMSAR member tonight, not being examined at an inquisition by two precocious kids.

"Maybe someday?" He glanced toward the stairs. How long did a diaper change take? "If I met the right person."

Two lines formed above Kendall's nose. "Leanne's nice. She's not married."

A twelve-year-old playing matchmaker. He shifted his weight between his feet. "Yeah, but we work together."

Both kids looked at him as if he'd grown a third eye and horns.

"Leanne and I are just friends," he clarified.

Austin sighed. "That's what Uncle Jake and Aunt Carly used to say, but the next thing you know, they're kissing."

Kendall nodded. "Then I got to be a flower girl at their wedding. And now we have a new cousin. Nicole is so cute."

That was okay if you wanted to be on the family plan; Christian preferred being single. Women always wanted something in return for loving you. They also wanted you to be someone you weren't.

Christian's gaze strayed to the front door. Okay, Thomas had warned him. But he hadn't expected all these personal questions. He needed to find a way to distract the kids. And fast.

The Christmas tree with twinkling multicolored lights, popcorn-and-cranberry strung garland, silver bells, gold balls and all sorts of one-of-a-kind ornaments caught his attention. "Nice tree."

"We cut it down ourselves," Austin announced.

"With help from our dad and Uncle Jake," Kendall added.

The house where Christian lived had no decorations. No tree. No wreath. No lights. But he and his roommates would put something up eventually.

Last year, Riley had found a Charlie Brown worthy tree two days before Christmas. They'd decorated it with chili pepper shaped lights, poker chips and playing cards. The angel on top had wings, but wasn't quite angelic looking with her ample hourglass figure.

Christian liked the Willinghams' tree better. "Who wants to tell me about the special ornaments on the tree?"

The kids rushed for the tree nearly knocking each other over in the rush to pick out an ornament.

He followed, a smile warming his heart.

Austin pointed to a teddy bear on a rocking horse. "This one is from when I was a baby. It was my first Christmas. But I don't remember it."

"What was all that noise?" a familiar feminine voice asked. "Did a herd of elephants stop by looking for some peanuts?"

Christian turned and sucked in a sharp breath.

Leanne stood on the bottom stair with a toddler in her arms. The boy sucked his right thumb and twirled the hair at the end of her braid with his left hand. A smudge of flour was on her cheek. More covered the front of her red-and-green apron, including two distinct kid-size handprints.

The little boy glanced up at her with total adoration. A wide smile broke across Thomas's face.

Christian's heart lurched. She looked like a…mom.

"I see you've met Kendall and Austin." Her tender gaze went to each one of the kids. "This is Tyler. He'll be two on December 23."

Tyler rested his head against Thomas's shoulder. He looked perfectly content cradled in her arms.

Lucky kid. Christian's stomach felt funny. Might have been the grande burrito from lunch.

Austin wrinkled his nose. "Does he still stink?"

"Nope," Thomas said. "He's all clean with a new diaper."

Austin exhaled loudly. "Thank goodness. Was it green?"

"Not this time," she said.

Thomas joined them in the living room. She wore no shoes, only socks. Colorful ones with stripes and polka dots. "So what's going on?"

"We're telling Christian about some of the ornaments." Kendall pointed to a pink-and-purple snowboard hanging from one of the branches. "This one is from Sean. He gave me the ornament and a matching board last Christmas."

"Me, too." Austin pointed out his blue-and-red snowboard ornament. "But Uncle Jake says we still have to keep skiing."

"Your uncle Jake is a smart man," Thomas said.

That sounded more like her. Good. Christian wasn't sure what to make of the motherly version when she always seemed so hard-nosed and detached at the station. This new side of her made him a little light-headed.

"It's easier to learn how to skin with skis," she continued. "You can always switch to a split board when you're older and know how to snowboard really well."

"The kids go into the back country?" Christian asked.

"They've gone a couple of times when the conditions were right," she said.

Kendall sighed. "I can't wait until I'm old enough to climb the mountain."

"A few more years, sweetie, then we will." Affection filled Thomas's voice. "I can't wait to see you standing on that summit. Just like your dad used to."

Dad equaled Nick. The guy must have been something special based on how everyone in OMSAR talked about him. But Thomas's sincerity and love for these kids left Christian feeling a little off balance. He sat on a nearby rocking chair.

Kendall beamed.

Tyler wiggled in her arms. "Dow-dow."

Thomas laughed. "Okay, big man, I'll put you down."

Amazing. Christian stared captivated. He'd watched her be sweet and gentle with Owen, but Christian never thought he would hear Thomas sound so nurturing. He didn't need mothering, but he wouldn't mind her caring for him like that.

As the kids pointed out special ornaments, he tried to reconcile the woman in front of him with the strong, athletic, badass he knew from the station, mountain rescue and back country skiing. Tried and failed.

He liked paramedic, mountain rescuer Thomas, but something about this Mother Earth Thomas appealed to him at a gut level. He didn't want a wife, but a fling sounded good.

She placed the boy on his feet, but didn't let go of him until she knew he was stable. "There you go, Tyler."

The kid toddled toward the tree. "Bah."

Christian watched Leanne follow after the kid. Not quite hovering, but close enough to catch if he fell. His sister, Brianna, did the same thing with his niece. Brianna was pregnant again, due on January 2. Her husband, Jeff, kept joking he wanted the baby to be born by the 31st for the tax write-off.

"Bah means box," Kendall translated. "Tyler likes boxes."

Austin nodded. "All of his *B* words sound the same."

"Just wait," Leanne said. "This time next year, Tyler will have a much bigger vocabulary."

A buzzer sounded from another room. It reminded him of an oven timer.

The kids cheered. Even little Tyler joined in.

Christian's gaze locked with Thomas's brown eyes. Something jolted inside him. Must be his lunch. "What's cooking?"

"A Yule Log," Kendall answered.

"What's that?" Christian asked.

Austin jumped up and down. "A special Christmas cake."

"It's also known as *Bûche de Noël*," Leanne explained.

Austin placed his palms together then spread them apart. "Imagine a giant Ho-Ho. Only better."

Christian laughed. "Better than a Ho-Ho, huh? That has to be a really special cake."

Enthusiastic nods answered him.

"Come on. We don't want the cake to overcook." Thomas motioned to Tyler. "Can you grab him for me, Welton?"

The toddler climbed over an upholstered ottoman as if it were a boulder project. A devilish grin lit up the kid's face.

"No problem," Christian said. "I've got the size advantage."

With that, she hurried to the kitchen. Austin and Kendall followed as if Leanne were the Pied Piper.

"Come on, bud." Christian swooped the kid into his arms. "Let's go."

Tyler twisted, kicked his legs and tried to get away.

"Sorry, little dude." Two sad hazel-green eyes met Christian's. The kid looked ready to cry or scream. "Failure is not an option. Don't even think about making me look bad in front of Thomas. Leanne. Got it?"

Tyler stared at Christian as if he were crazy.

Yeah, rationalizing with a two-year-old wasn't the smartest thing he'd ever done, but the kid wasn't struggling or crying.

"Let's go see the cake," he said.

"Cake."

Christian laughed. "Hey, you said that word perfectly."

"Cake," Tyler repeated.

"Everything okay out there?" Thomas yelled.

"Fine." Christian lowered his voice. He looked at Tyler. "Come on. We'd better get in there before she sends out a search party."

CHAPTER EIGHT

LAUGHTER drowned out the Christmas music playing on the kitchen's iPod docking stereo. Leanne whipped more cream. She loved babysitting these three kids. The older two reminded her so much of her friend Nick. Kendall had inherited his have-no-fear personality. Austin looked like a mini version of his dad and had the same sense of humor.

Christian sat at the kitchen table and held Tyler on his lap. The two seemed so natural together, as if they did this every day. Unexpected, but so appealing.

Leanne could imagine Christian as a father, something she'd never thought of him as before. It took every ounce of strength not to pull out her cell phone to take a picture.

He met her gaze. "Now I see why you like babysitting."

Leanne's heart squeezed tight. "Fun times."

Austin showed off his latest hip-hop moves holding a spatula in his hand that he used as a microphone to sing "Rocking Around the Christmas Tree." Kendall sat at the table and concentrated on spreading the filling over the chocolate cake. Tyler licked a spoon covered with whipped cream.

A warm and fuzzy feeling enveloped Leanne, as comforting as a cup of hot chocolate after a day on the hill. She'd expected chaos with Welton here, but instead it almost felt as if they were a...

Family.

"You're doing great, Kendall." Christian acted like a big kid at the station, sometimes giving Paulson a run at the most immature title, but he knew how to interact with kids. Even little Tyler, who was a handful under the best of circumstances, seemed enchanted by the playful firefighter. "Remember what Leanne said. Spread the filling to a half inch of the edge."

Falling under Welton's spell would be so easy to do. Easy, Leanne reminded herself, but stupid. They worked the same shift at the only fire station in town. He dated more than one woman at once. Commitment was so clearly not his thing. But she couldn't deny her attraction.

Any woman with a pulse wouldn't be able to do that. Especially after seeing him interact with the kids. Her heart sighed.

Kendall added more whipped-cream filling to her spatula and layered it on the cake. "Like this, Christian?"

"Exactly," he said with a tender smile that could melt the thickest glacier.

Leanne swallowed and looked away.

Austin licked the homemade whipped cream off a spoon like Tyler.

Christian laughed. "Austin, dude, make sure you leave some for the cake."

"Is the chocolate frosting ready?" Kendall asked with an expectant look on her face.

"We'll make that after we roll the cake and are waiting for it to chill in the refrigerator," Leanne explained. "Don't forget we still have to eat dinner."

Tyler used his spoon to feed whipped cream to Christian. "Din-din."

None made it into Christian's mouth, but was smeared over his face instead.

Leanne chuckled.

He grinned, his straight white teeth surrounded by the whipped cream on his lips and mouth. "Thanks, little dude."

"Mo," Tyler said.

Christian laughed. "No more."

Austin scrunched his nose. "You look like a snowman."

"Or Santa Claus," Kendall offered. "The whipped cream looks like a white beard."

Leanne appreciated Christian being such a good sport about it. She grabbed a handful of napkins and handed them to him.

"Can we tell you what we want for Christmas, Santa?" Austin teased.

"Sure," Christian said. "If Santa can get a few more napkins first."

Tyler wanted to help make an even better mess. His little hands grabbed at the napkins.

"This isn't working," Christian said.

Austin giggled. "No, it's not. But you sure look funny."

"That's not nice," Kendall scolded.

"But he does," Austin countered.

Kendall nodded.

Leanne grabbed a roll of paper towels. "You hold Tyler so he can't help. And I'll wipe."

Christian's gaze met her. "Thanks."

Her mouth went dry. "I haven't done anything yet."

"It's the thought that counts."

He gave Tyler his car keys to keep the toddler's hands occupied during the cleanup. Smart man.

She ripped off several sheets. "This won't take long."

"I don't mind," Christian said in a husky tone that sent a shiver down her spine.

"You're a good sport."

As she brought the paper towel to his face, her pulse sped up like an out-of-control semitruck that lost its brakes coming down Highway 26. An odd reaction. This wasn't the first time she'd cleaned up one of the guys from the station or rescue team. This was no different than helping a climbing or ski partner, either. Well, except blood wasn't involved. Whipped cream was.

Leanne ran the paper towel over his face. Smooth. No razor stubble. She preferred the clean-cut look that most of the firefighters, including Welton, sported. The only time she'd seen him unshaven was when she found him in the snow cave or when he first woke up on their shift. The early-morning stubble did look sexy and bad boyish.

His gaze met hers again.

"Almost finished," she said.

"You missed under his chin and by his nose," Austin said.

"Yes, I did." She broke eye contact with Christian, tossed the first paper towels then grabbed more. "There's a lot of whipped cream here."

"Such a waste." Christian raised a brow. "I can think of some much better uses for it."

So could Leanne.

Fluffy, yummy, sexy. Lots of different uses for whipped cream popped into her mind. None of them rated G.

She fought the urge to fan herself. When had it gotten so hot in here?

Too bad Welton wasn't interested in dating past Monday.

Wait a sec. She wasn't looking to date him.

"The whipped cream should be on the cake," Kendall said.

Thank you, Kendall. Leanne's mind had been going elsewhere. Time to focus. The sooner she finished, the better.

Wiping Welton's face felt different than cleaning up a co-worker, team member or climbing partner. Intimate. Even with three pint-size chaperones.

Worse, she liked it. Liked cleaning him up. Liked being close enough to smell the scent of his soap and shampoo.

Uh-oh. Better get some distance. Fast.

"There." Leanne wiped off the last bit from Christian's face. She balled the napkin so the whipped cream was trapped inside. As she tossed the paper towels into the garbage can, her hands shook. She pressed them against her sides. "All done."

"Yep," Austin agreed. "You got it all."

Kendall nodded.

Christian's gaze remained on Leanne. "You're going to have to let me return the favor."

Her stomach tingled. The look he gave her. His saying her

name… She couldn't have responded even if she'd known what to say.

Kendall scraped the bowl of whipped cream with her spatula. "No worries. There's enough to finish the cake."

Leanne forced herself to look away. She wiped her hands. "You're right, Kendall. Spread the rest of the filling while I take Tyler upstairs to change his clothes."

Christian stood with a whipped-cream-covered Tyler in his arms. "Do you want me to take him up?"

Leanne met them in the doorway. She held out her arms. Tyler went to her without any fuss. "Thanks, but I know where everything is."

"I'll supervise these two."

The older kids cheered.

"You have a fan club," Leanne said.

Amusement gleamed in Christian's eyes. "The more members the merrier."

Very charming. She would give him that. "We'll be back."

"Wait." Austin pointed at the kitchen doorway. "You're standing under the mistletoe."

Leanne glanced up. Sprigs of mistletoe with holly berries hung from a red ribbon attached to the top of the doorway with a thumbtack. She kissed Tyler's forehead. "A mistletoe kiss for my favorite almost two-year-old."

"Don't forget Christian," Kendall said.

"Yeah." His eyes filled with mischief. "Your favorite firefighter needs a kiss under the mistletoe."

Leanne inhaled sharply. A kiss sounded like a bad idea. If only because the thought of kissing him appealed to her.

"You have to kiss," Austin urged. "It's tradition."

"I'm all for tradition." Christian looked at Leanne. "What about you?"

"Oh, she's all for tradition, too," Kendall said with certainty. "Isn't that right?"

"Yes." Leanne lowered her voice to a mere whisper. "This is only for the kids. Got it?"

Christian nodded once.

She rose up on her tiptoes to kiss his cheek. As she neared his face, Christian turned his head. Her mouth landed right on his lips.

Something sparked. Static electricity? Leanne had no idea. She only knew his kiss was hot, oh-so-very hot. It burned, but in a very good way.

His lips moved over hers as if they'd done it a million times, but she'd never been kissed so thoroughly in her entire life. Heat rushed through her veins. Her heart rate quadrupled.

Something touched her face. Sweet, sticky.

Her eyelids flew open.

Tyler.

Oh, no. No. She jerked away from Christian. Welton. What had she done?

The surprise in his eyes matched the way she felt inside. She looked at the kids at the table. Big grins lit up their faces. "Satisfied?"

They both nodded.

"Well, I'm not," Christian whispered.

"Too bad," she whispered back. "You were only supposed to get a peck on the cheek."

"I knew you were going to say that." Amusement laced each word. He would think this was funny. Darn him. "But a kiss on the cheek isn't in the spirit of the mistletoe tradition. It's more like sticking your tongue out at it."

All three kids stuck out their tongues.

Leanne laughed, a mix of nerves and wanting to pretend what happened hadn't meant anything when her lips still throbbed. She fought the urge to touch her mouth.

The older two kids were distracted as a new song came on. They sang along at the top of their lungs. Tyler clapped along.

"Well," she whispered to Christian. "Sticking my tongue out is better than sticking it down your throat."

"Sure about that?" His warm breath fanned her neck. "Maybe we should find out?"

Anticipation hummed through Leanne.

Heaven help her, but her lips wanted more of Welton's kisses. Worse, she was tempted to see if it was better or not.

She swallowed around the lump in her throat.

So not good.

Hours later, the kids were nestled in their beds. Christmas carols continued to play. Logs crackled in the fire. Two cups of hot chocolate sat on the coffee table.

A great night. Especially with Leanne setting next to him on the couch. She'd long since removed the apron and washed off the flour smudges.

But all he wanted to think about was her rock-his-world kiss.

Leanne kissed as well as she did everything else. She tasted so sweet and warm. Sugar and spice and everything nice. A way he hadn't expected. He wanted another taste. Without three kids watching them.

But she wanted only to work on the event.

Fine. But once they finished he wanted to get back to what they'd started in the kitchen. Even if it meant bringing the mistletoe into the living room.

"Donations for the toy drive are still low." Her laptop rested on top of her jean-covered thighs. He preferred her in well-worn jeans that accentuated the curve of her hips and a sweater that fit tight across her chest to the unisex fire station uniform.

She stared at the monitor. "But even with these conservative estimates for the dinner and silent auction, it looks like this should bring in much needed funds for OMSAR."

"You sound surprised every time it looks like the Christmas Magic celebration might be a success."

"That's to offset you," she said. "Your confidence never wavers."

"Not about this."

Curiosity shone in her eyes. "About what then?"

Damn. Christian had left that door wide-open. He searched for a noncommittal way to answer. "A few things."

"That many, huh?"

He shrugged, half laughed, wondered how he could change the subject.

"What are they?" she asked.

Christian hesitated. He wasn't one to admit weakness, but this wasn't just any woman. If he wanted to get to know her better—he did—and kiss her again—he really wanted to—he needed to talk to her. Openly. Honestly. Not something he was used to doing. He dragged his hand through his hair. "Remember when I told you about my climbing road trip?"

"Eighteen months climbing and living like a dirtbag to figure out what was important to you."

He nodded. "At the beginning of that trip my confidence wavered big-time. My family didn't want me to go. Neither did my girlfriend."

"You didn't want her to go with you?"

His collar tightened around his throat. "She didn't want to come."

"That had to be tough."

"I kept wondering if I'd made the right decision to go. If I should have stayed at the winery and got engaged instead."

"Engaged." Leanne sounded surprised. "It must have been serious."

"The most serious I've ever been." He hadn't thought of Kelly in a couple of years. "We met at OSU. We were both taking Enology and Viticulture courses. Fell in love over winemaking."

"Was the road trip the right decision?" Leanne asked.

"Definitely," he said without any hesitation. "I met amazing people and learned a lot about myself. I'd do it again in a heartbeat."

"Sounds like a trip of a lifetime."

"It was."

"What about the girlfriend? Regrets?"

"None. She didn't really love me," Christian explained. "She wanted the lifestyle being a Welton could give her and her winemaking. When I wasn't sure that was the future I wanted, she didn't want me."

"Ouch."

Kelly wanted to trade her love for a life that wasn't right for him. She was one more in a line of women who always wanted something from him that he couldn't give. The same as his family. "I got over it."

"And the other time…"

"You really want to know?" he asked.

"I do," she said. "We haven't spent a lot of time together outside of the station except for working on the celebration."

"We've backcountry skied together and babysat." And kissed.

His gazed lowered to her lips. He really wanted to kiss her again.

"Please," she said.

If only she was asking for another kiss… Christian took a deep breath. "It was on the mountain with Owen. He had more experience. All the experience. I wasn't sure I could build the snow cave right and fast enough with the storm on top of us. I'd only practiced once before. It was like starting all over as a rookie again. I was out of my element up there. I knew if I failed we would die."

There. He'd said it. Christian expected to see pity, even disgust from Thomas.

Instead her eyes softened, full of compassion. She touched his arm. "You didn't fail. You'd practiced. Many people don't even do that. You knew what you had to do and did it. You saved both your and your cousin's lives. You did well, Christian. I'd tie-in with you anytime."

Warmth flowed through him. Her hand remained on his arm, but it wasn't enough. He wanted to reach out to her, to draw her closer to him, but he hesitated.

She'd said the kiss under the mistletoe had been for the kids. Yet she'd kissed him back. Hard. That couldn't have been for the kids' sake. But for hers. And his.

Still he didn't want to make a move only to be shut down. Not with so much event planning they still had to do. Best to stop thinking about kissing her.

"Anyone would have had doubts in a situation like that," she added.

"You?"

"Heck, yeah," she admitted. "Having a lot of experience doesn't mean you know everything. Or aren't afraid."

"I never thought I'd hear you say that."

"Well, if you tell anyone I'll deny I said it." She winked. "I have a reputation to uphold."

"One of the guys."

Thomas nodded once, but she looked uncomfortable. "So..."

"So I told you mine, you tell me yours."

Her brows furrowed. "Mine?"

"When your confidence wavered or when you were afraid."

"We'd be here all night."

Christian liked spending time with Leanne, more so than any woman he'd dated in a long time. Maybe...ever. "I wouldn't mind."

"Hannah and Garrett might."

"They aren't home yet."

Leanne took a deep breath and exhaled slowly. "There was this one time on Stuart."

"Mount Stuart in Washington?" Christian asked.

She nodded. "It was sunny. Only a few clouds in the sky. Good conditions for a day climb on the West Ridge. About half-way up the weather pattern changed. It was so strange. Rain, hail, snow, sun again. We should have turned around, but we were young with one goal, the summit, so kept climbing."

"We?"

"Paulson and I." She remembered the climb as if it was yesterday, not twelve years ago. "We reached the summit and started our descent, but daylight disappeared so fast. I couldn't see the route. Neither of us was really sure where we were. Turns out we'd gotten into Ulrich's Coulior instead of the Cascadian. We ended up stuck on this narrow ledge. It downsloped so much I kept thinking I was going to slide off. We had belay jackets, but no sleeping bags or bivy sacks. The "ten essentials" were more like "ten suggestions" to us back then. I sat on my pack and my feet dangled over the edge. They were so cold, but there was really no place for them. I tried curling up in the fetal position. Paulson cuddled against me. It took a real effort to stay like that, but at least one side of us was warmer."

She tried to sound lighthearted, but Christian had done enough climbing to know being stuck out in the elements overnight was not a situation anyone wanted to be in. At least he and Owen had had a snow cave to take shelter in. "How did the night go?"

"Uncomfortable doesn't begin to describe what we went through. We kept our harnesses on and anchored ourselves as best we could. It was freezing cold. The temperature kept dropping. I shivered so badly my helmet sounded like a jackhammer against the rock behind me. We shared one of those space blankets. Neither of us wanted to fall asleep. We kept slapping each other and ourselves to stay awake and warm. Paulson and I both knew if it snowed or rained again, we would be dead. But neither of us said a word to the other. I know I didn't. I was afraid of jinxing us."

Christian placed his arm around the back of the sofa, careful to avoid her shoulders. It was the only way to get closer to her without physically touching her. "You're here, so you made it down."

She nodded. "The night seemed to last forever, but finally the sun peeked over the ridgeline. It was so beautiful to see the dawn break. As soon as there was enough light, we started our descent and figured out where we'd gone wrong. An hour later, snow started falling, but we were moving and warmer by then."

"You were lucky."

Another nod. "Learning when to turn around greatly reduced my future unplanned bivvies. Paulson's still working on that one. He and Cocoa ended up stuck in a snow cave on Hood. Though part of me thinks Paulson did that on purpose."

Christian laughed. "I wouldn't put it past him."

"Cocoa didn't seem to mind much, either."

"What about you? Did you mind them bivying?"

Leanne's forehead wrinkled. "Why would I mind?"

"You and Paulson must have gotten friendly on that ledge."

"What happens on bivy ledges stays there. Paulson and I only did what we had to do to stay warm," she explained. "If anything, our unplanned bivies over the years made it clear we should be only friends if that's what you were getting at."

"It was."

"You're sure curious about me and Paulson."

Christian shrugged. "It's hard to believe you're just friends."

"Believe it. Paulson sees me like his little sister. We can't take each other seriously most of the time." She sounded irritated. Christian didn't blame her. He shouldn't care. It's not like he wanted anything more than a fling with her. Who she dated didn't matter.

"Did we get to everything about the celebration you wanted to cover?" she asked.

"Yes."

She closed the laptop. "Thanks for coming over here tonight."

"That sounds like a good-night."

"We're finished talking business."

"We could talk about other stuff," he offered.

"It's your night off. Tomorrow we have to meet with the others about the dinner and auction," she said. "It's kind of late, but you could still hit the brewpub."

He didn't want to go anywhere. "I don't mind keeping you company."

"Hannah and Garrett should be finished Christmas shopping soon."

"We still have a little time to head back into the kitchen and stand under the mistletoe," he half joked.

She laughed, but wouldn't meet his eyes. "We could, but we both know why we can't."

He recognized that serious, all-business tone. "It's not official fire-and-rescue policy that employees can't date."

"No, but it's my policy." Her eyes darkened. "And be real, Welton, you don't want to date me."

"Okay, I don't," he admitted. "I don't want to date anybody right now, but I want to kiss you."

"I appreciate your honesty. But I told you the only reason we kissed. Tradition is very important to the kids," she explained. "The kiss was…nice. Let's leave it as that."

"The kiss was hot. And I don't want to leave it."

The song "All I Want for Christmas" played on the radio. Christian knew what he wanted.

Leanne turned to face him. "The truth is, Christian, even if you weren't a firefighter, I wouldn't kiss you again. You and I are very different."

"I'm younger."

"It's more than an age thing. I haven't dated in a while, but when I do I know exactly what I want."

"What's that?" he asked.

"Not a casual date or a fling. I want a real relationship. A serious one. Something that will last a very long time."

"I appreciate your honesty." That kind of relationship was the last thing he wanted. Still Christian couldn't forget how her kisses made him feel, how much he enjoyed being with her and talking to her. He leaned toward Leanne. "We could always share a few kisses until you're ready to find what you're looking for."

"That wouldn't be a good idea."

She backed away, but not before he glimpsed the longing in her dark chocolate eyes.

A-ha. "You want me to kiss you."

Leanne stared at the Christmas tree. "Don't complicate things, Welton."

She hadn't said no. That meant yes. A smug smile settled on his lips. "Kisses won't complicate anything."

"We don't want the same things."

"True, but that doesn't mean we can't have a little fun in the meantime."

She wouldn't meet his eyes.

"I am going to kiss you again, Leanne Thomas," he said. "Even if it means I have to buy all the mistletoe in Hood Hamlet to do it."

"Please…"

"Kiss you," he offered.

"Don't do anything embarrassing." Her gaze implored him. "I'd rather keep this between you and me."

"And the kids?"

She ignored his quip. "You might not care about your reputation, but I care about mine."

Her words felt like a slap to his face. "I would never do anything to hurt you."

Doubt filled her eyes.

His insides twisted. He wanted her to believe him. "I wouldn't."

"Then stop talking about kissing me again, okay?"

"Okay." The last thing he wanted to do was upset her. "I won't bring it up again."

And he wouldn't.

But if she gave him any indication she wanted another kiss, he was going to be all over it. All over her.

CHAPTER NINE

SUNDAY morning, Leanne entered the station ready to work. She wanted something to do other than sit around her house thinking about kissing Christian. She'd been so preoccupied by him she hadn't done more than string the lights on her Christmas tree.

Pathetic.

I am going to kiss you again, Leanne Thomas. Even if it means I have to buy all the mistletoe in Hood Hamlet to do it.

Romantic, no doubt. No wonder so many women wanted to date Welton. He said the words they wanted to hear. Not even she was as immune as she'd like to be. Her lips tingled with anticipation thinking about more kisses.

But all Christian wanted was kisses. Strike that. He probably wanted more, whatever he could get in the moment. But nothing…else.

No relationship. No commitment. No love. No thank you!

When she got involved again, Leanne knew what she wanted—everything he didn't. She should be relieved.

Leanne walked into the garage. Besides, a relationship with someone at the station, someone who worked her same shift, wasn't a smart idea. It wasn't against the rules, but highly discouraged. Still, a part of her was disappointed she'd scared him off so easily by saying she wanted a serious relationship.

Her gaze landed on Christian. She pulled up short.

He leaned against the back wall of the station bays, looking gorgeous in his blue uniform and neatly-styled hair.

Her pulse rocketed.

Okay, she had a crush on him. On a younger man. Did that make her a cougar?

His intense blue eyes studied her. "Good morning, Thomas."

Not Leanne. She reminded herself that was how she wanted it. "Welton."

"How's the toy drive looking?" he asked.

Yesterday, he'd sent a text message telling her not to come to the meeting. She could work on the toy drive while he handled the event planning. She'd appreciated that. Though she'd missed being a part of the get-together. All her friends were attending. Many of the town's business owners.

Who was she kidding? She'd missed Christian. Stupid.

"The library barrel had a few toys," she said. "Donations are still way down."

"We'll get plenty of toys at the dinner."

"Hope so." His confidence appealed to her. "The morning briefing…"

"We have a couple of minutes." He straightened. "I have good news about the dinner."

They wanted to attract sponsors to offset some of the expenses. "Did someone buy a table?"

"Better than that." He grinned. "My grandfather called. Welton Winery is going to underwrite the entire dinner and silent auction. My family is going to attend, too."

Her mouth gaped. "That means…"

"No expenses," Christian finished for her. "Whatever money we raise goes directly to OMSAR."

This was exactly what the unit needed to pay for new equipment and training, except…

His brows furrowed. "I thought you'd be happy."

"I am, but I don't want you to be pressured into doing something you don't want to do in order to help OMSAR. If there are strings attached to your grandfather's offer…?"

Christian's eyes softened. "No strings. I made sure. But I appreciate you…"

Something passed between them again. A look. A connection. Leanne held her breath.

"…asking," he said finally.

"Thank-you." Her voice sounded husky. "And your grandfather."

"This is because of what you, the rescue team and all of OMSAR did for me and Owen. Thank yourselves."

Excitement rocketed through her. This was going to make such a big difference for the unit. Part of her felt like twirling around. But one thought kept her from wanting to celebrate. "This is going to sound bad, probably really bad, but given how things are turning out, I'm kind of glad you and Owen needed to be rescued."

Christian gave a laugh. "You know, Thomas, I feel the same way."

At least she wasn't the only one. Leanne motioned to the doorway. "Morning briefing."

"Ladies, first."

"One of the guys, remember?" she teased.

"Yeah, I remember." Christian didn't sound too happy about it, but he walked in front of her. "But you should remember there's nothing wrong with being one of the girls."

Leanne stood in the doorway a bit stunned. No one at the station had ever said that to her. No one at OMSAR, either.

This was a man's world. She wanted—needed—to fit in. Didn't Christian understand that?

Of course not. He was a guy.

Leanne entered the briefing room. Her gaze shot to Christian. He was a guy who would be kissing someone on New Year's Eve. Alexa or Rachel or another woman. Maybe Leanne should be one of the girls and find a man to kiss, too. But the thought of kissing a guy who wasn't Christian seemed annoyingly unappealing…unsatisfying. She plopped into the closest chair.

The lieutenant cleared his throat and ran through the briefing. Nothing too out of the ordinary, except more physical training. Leanne liked the new workout, but not everyone agreed.

"Before I forget," the lieutenant added. "There's a full moon tonight so you know what that means."

"The crazies will be out," Paulson said.

She forced herself not to look at Christian. "And anything can happen."

At two o'clock in the morning, on fire attack, Christian headed toward the house fire with a hose line. He wore his full turnouts and a SCBA—Self-Contained Breathing Apparatus. The smoke wasn't dark or breathing around the doors and windows. No sign of a possible backdraft situation.

He entered through the front door and remembered something from fire academy.

Right wall in. Left wall out.

Dark. He couldn't see a thing. No dim orange glow.

He listened. That was when he heard it. The familiar crackling of fire and burning.

Paulson, Baer, a longtime volunteer firefighter, and Keller followed Christian.

Smoke billowed, filling the doorway out of the living room. He couldn't see out of his mask very well.

As Christian moved to the doorway, the noise and heat increased. Orange. He opened the hose nozzle.

Flames licked the ceiling. With Keller behind him, Christian aimed the hose to douse them and other hot spots. They needed to get to the stairs.

One adult and child were outside being treated for smoke inhalation by Thomas and O'Ryan. Another adult and child were unaccounted for. Still in the house. Somewhere.

Paulson carried an ax. He'd searched the downstairs with Baer. "They have to be upstairs."

They attacked the fire on the way up. The higher they went, the thicker the smoke. Visibility decreased more.

Christian aimed the nozzle at the flames, but the fire didn't want to die.

"Help!" Coughs followed the cry.

Water from the hose cleared the path toward the sound.

"We've lost the garage," a voice said over the radio. "Find them and get out."

A door was ajar. No flames. No heat. But smoke filled the room.

Christian readied the hose. Paulson opened the door. The four of them entered.

In the darkness, figures lay on the floor. A man. A child. Gasping for breath, coughing, alive.

Paulson scooped up a little girl wearing a pink nightgown. She struggled against him with frightened eyes. "Kitty."

Baer helped the man.

He coughed. "Can't find Tinkerbell. Kitten. In here somewhere."

"Do you have everyone?" the lieutenant asked.

"Yes," Keller replied.

Not everybody. Christian thought about the little girl's kitten.

"We're starting to lose the house. Evacuate the structure."

As Christian stepped out of the bedroom, he remembered the fear in the little girl's eyes and voice. This family was going to lose everything right before Christmas. He didn't want them to lose the kitten, too.

"Welton," Keller called.

"Take the hose," Christian said. "I'll be right behind you."

A firefighter never went into a fire or stayed in alone. But orders and regulations wouldn't mean anything to that family, especially the little girl. All Christian needed was sixty more seconds to find the cat.

Animals got scared and usually hid in situations like this. The room wasn't that big. He checked under the bed, behind the dresser and in the closet.

The smoke thickened. The heat intensified.

Thirty more seconds. He pushed aside a toy box. The kitten wasn't underneath.

"Welton."

He ignored the call over the radio. Fifteen seconds.

Leanne's smiling face appeared front and center in his mind. But she was outside. Safe. Christian didn't need to worry about her. He had to find the little girl's kitten. Tinkerbell.

"Get out, Welton," the lieutenant ordered. "Now."

A two-story dollhouse sat a few inches away from the wall. He pulled it out. Inside one of the rooms lay a small, gray kitten. Unconscious.

Damn.

Flames covered the doorway and spread to the ceiling. He slipped the kitten into his pocket.

"Welton." The lieutenant did not sound happy. "Retreat. That's an order."

"Got the cat," Christian replied. "Unconscious."

Heat surrounded him. Flames, too. Noise roared.

Something in the hallway collapsed. They weren't losing the house. They'd lost it. The structure was failing. And he was trapped.

He thought about Leanne, about wanting to hold her one more time, gaze into her brown eyes and kiss her. Time to get the hell out of here so he could do that.

Christian opened the window and pushed out the screen. Lights from the engine flashed. Firefighters aimed hoses and sprayed water. Not for the house, the structure was a lost cause, but for him.

"Bailing out the window," he said into the radio.

He grabbed his escape kit, one of the newer pieces of gear they'd started carrying for self-rescue, and anchored the rope to the window frame. As the flames danced toward him, he climbed out and rappelled down the rope. He ran from the burning house.

Leanne met him halfway across the yard. Worry filled her pretty brown eyes. "Christian…"

He pulled the kitten out of his pocket and placed the limp animal onto her hands.

She checked the cat. "It's not breathing."

He hadn't been able to tell with his mask and all the smoke. As she began mouth-to-mouth, he ripped off his mask.

Leanne hurried to the medical gear. Christian followed.

"Tinkerbell," the little girl cried. Thankfully the mother held her back.

"Come on, Tinkerbell," he said. "Breathe, kitty."

Leanne kept working on the kitten. Finally she looked at him. "Tinkerbell's breathing."

Relief washed over him.

Leanne placed an oxygen mask near the kitten's face. "You could have been killed."

She sounded tense, scared. "I knew I could find the cat."

She continued giving the kitten some blow by oxygen. "You were ordered to retreat."

"I'm sure I'll be reprimanded."

"And rightly so. That was an incredibly reckless thing to do." The kitten perked up. "An incredibly brave thing, too."

He smiled at her compliment. "For the record, I wasn't trying to impress you this time."

Leanne's gaze met his. She looked at him the way he'd pictured her when he was inside the burning house. Smiling. Beautiful. His. "Well, you did."

Christian's heart thudded. He wanted nothing more than to kiss her right now.

The kitten squirmed. *"Mew."*

She placed the cat in Christian's gloved hands. "Take Tinkerbell over to the little girl."

"Me?"

"You found the cat. That makes you the hero."

"I'm not—"

"Go." Pride filled Leanne's eyes. "You earned this."

Christian handed the wiggly kitten to the little girl now wrapped in a blanket. Someone snapped a picture.

She hugged him. "Thank you, Mr. Fireman."

Another flash lit up the night sky.

Neighbors surrounded the family. Someone clapped. Others cheered. Everyone joined in.

He nodded his appreciation then made his way back to the engine.

A muscle throbbed on the lieutenant's jaw. "We'll talk about this at the station."

"Yes, sir."

With that the lieutenant walked away.

Paulson slapped Christian on the back. "Well done, Welton."

"Thomas got the cat breathing."

"She couldn't have done that if you hadn't found Tinkerbell," Paulson said. "Don't mind the lieutenant. It's his job to make sure we all make it out safely. I'm sure you gave him a few gray hairs tonight."

"Not the intention."

"He knows that, rookie. Even if he won't admit it."

Christian glanced over at Leanne. He'd never seen that kind of worry in her eyes. Had it been for him?

A smile tugged at the corners of his lips thinking it might have been. Maybe he would get more kisses, after all.

"She's upset, too," Paulson said. "You know Thomas. Always a stickler for rules."

Christian's gaze remained on her as she packed up her equipment. "Yeah, but that's what makes her who she is."

"You're right about that." Paulson stared at Leanne, too. "She's tough and strong and totally self-reliant. I pity the fool who falls in love with her."

Christian nodded, but had a sinking feeling in the pit of his stomach. "Me, too."

Later that afternoon, Leanne glanced at the clock on her microwave. Christian was supposed to stop by to help her with the dinner program and auction catalogs. They hadn't set a firm time. She wished they had.

Ever since the house fire, she'd been on edge. She'd always been able to detach from what was going on with her coworkers on a call. Not this morning. Fear had gripped her heart when Christian hadn't exited the house with the others. She'd thought he was lost until he rappelled from the second story window like a superhero. Her relief had been palpable. And that's when she knew…

She cared about him.

Not like Paulson or Hughes or Porter or Moreno. Not like any of her fellow firefighters or OMSAR team.

Leanne had feelings, deep feelings, for Christian. Ones that couldn't go anywhere. Ones she would have to ignore. For the sake of the fire station. For the safety of her heart.

Once the Christmas celebration was over, it would be easier. Until then, she would…survive.

The doorbell rang.

She ran down the staircase and opened the door.

Christian stood on her porch. He held a red poinsettia plant. Behind him snow fell from the sky. "This is for you. I know all our work on the event has kept you from decorating."

Leanne's heart melted. If only… Nope. She knew better than to fantasize over something that wasn't going to happen. She took the plant. "Thanks."

He went upstairs.

She followed and set the plant on the breakfast bar. "I've got everything ready to collate."

"Let's hit it."

Time flew by. Leanne sat on her living room floor with Christian across from. They inserted the programs into each of the catalogs and clipped a bid number to the front. "This is my last one."

"Two more to go for me." A minute later, he placed his stack of catalogs in a box. "That's it."

"I can't believe how many catalogs there are."

"Carly said tickets sales have been brisk," Christian said.

"We should be set for the toy drive. We might even have enough donations to pass on to other organizations."

"Don't get ahead of yourself just yet." She placed lids on the boxes. "Let's wait to see how many toys are donated first."

His gaze racked over her. "So cautious for someone who takes risks every day?"

He was one to talk after this morning. "This is a different kind of risk."

"How so?" he asked.

"On the mountain skiing or climbing, it's an individual risk. Or you and your partner taking the risks together."

"Not if you're on a rescue."

"Then the team leader assesses the risk, too. The same way the lieutenant or the chief does on a call. But this celebration…" The weight of the boxes seemed to press down on her shoulders. "It feels as if all of Hood Hamlet is counting on this to save Christmas. If the event fails…"

"Christmas will survive no matter what happens. But I have a feeling it's going to be a huge success," he said. "What's left on the To Do list?"

She scanned the list. "Nothing. We get the rest of the night off. Now I can finally decorate my tree."

"Want some help?" he offered.

Temptation flared. She would love him to help her. But did she dare say yes? "I'm sure you have something better to do."

"I want to help you."

Last year she'd been alone at Christmastime for the first time in three years. Decorating the tree by herself had been a chore, not fun. She didn't relish the thought of a repeat performance this year.

"What do you say?" he pressed.

Having Christian trim the tree with her wasn't the same as kissing under the mistletoe. He wouldn't be kissing her again. He'd given his word. She would be safe having him keep her company. "Sure," she said finally. "I'd love the help."

* * *

Christmas carols played on the stereo. Flames crackled in the fireplace. Rubber boxes filled with ornaments neatly separated by cardboard sat on the living room floor. The only thing missing was…mistletoe.

Christian pushed that thought aside. Leanne wanted a boyfriend. He didn't want a girlfriend. Best to keep things platonic. No matter how sexy she looked in her tight-fitting jeans and turtleneck. Or the way she kept glancing his way.

He removed a paper star ornament. Gold-and-silver sparkles covered one side. The name LeLe was scrawled in a child's writing on the other. He remembered someone mentioning the nickname at the brewpub.

He held up the star by the attached gold ribbon. "Did you make this?"

"When I was seven." Leanne hung a red ball on the tree. "I have lots of ornaments from when I was growing up."

He placed the star on the tree. "You really do like Christmas."

She nodded.

"So Christmas magic—"

"I prefer Christmas spirit," she interrupted. "Magic implies some supernatural force that makes everything okay. Bad things happen this time of year, so does that mean that Christmas magic is only for some people? That doesn't seem fair."

He returned to the box. "I see your point, but it's still a nice thought."

Leanne shrugged.

Christian pulled out a frame made out of Popsicle sticks. The picture showed three children. Two teenage boys and a younger girl dressed head to toe in pink. The back read Cole (13), Troy (11) and LeLe (6). "Are these friends of yours?"

She took the ornament and stared at the picture. Her soft smile took Christian's breath away, but sadness filled her eyes, the way it had during the news interview with Rachel.

"My brothers." Leanne hung the frame on the tree right in the front. "I had two older brothers."

Had. Past tense. Christian didn't know what to say.

Leanne took another ornament out of the box.

"What happened?" he asked.

"A car accident." She hung a silver bell on a branch. "Black ice. Head-on collision."

No wonder the accident last week had affected her. Leanne reached for another ornament, but Christian touched her arm. "Wait a minute, okay?"

Leanne nodded.

"How old were your brothers?"

"Fourteen and sixteen." She pointed to a picture on the bookcase. A family portrait. Christian hadn't noticed it before. The little girl had curly ringlets, pink ribbons in her hair and a frilly pink dress. It looked nothing like Leanne. "That was taken a few months before the accident."

Such big smiles. Happy eyes. Christian remembered when his dad died suddenly. He never thought he'd feel happy again. "You must have been young."

"Nine."

"What about your parents?"

"They were killed, too."

He winced. His mother had taken off when he was twelve. His dad passed when he was twenty. But Christian couldn't imagine losing both parents when he was nine. "I had no idea."

She shrugged. "Everyone around here knew because of the stories in the newspaper. I saw therapists and grief counselors for years. But no matter what I said, my family wasn't coming back. So I stopped talking about it."

Always so tough. On the outside at least. Christian squeezed her arm. "Leanne, I'm so sorry."

She picked up another ornament, an angel. "Thanks."

Feathers covered the wing. Gold braided thread made the halo. The sweet face reminded him of Leanne. "At least you weren't with them."

"I was in the car." Her lower lip quivered. "I was the only survivor. Everybody else died. It was…"

He recognized the faraway look in her eyes. He'd seen it in his own reflection after his father died.

Christian took the angel out of her hand and carefully placed it back in the box. He led her to the couch and pulled her down to sit next to him. "Sit for a minute. You don't have to tell me anything."

"I want to." She stared at the photograph in the bookcase. "We were on our way home from my grandparents' house. It was late afternoon. We'd had an early supper. I was in the backseat. My brothers were on either side of me. I was playing with a new doll I'd just gotten."

She closed her eyes. Willing herself to remember or wanting to forget? Christian stroked her hand with his thumb.

"My mother screamed. She sounded so scared. Headlights were coming straight at us. My dad yelled. My brothers leaned over me. Covering me. Protecting me like they always did." Leanne grimaced. "And then that sound. The crunching. Jerking. Glass breaking. Spinning. It went on forever."

She trembled.

Christian let go of Leanne's hand, wrapped his arm around her and pulled her against him. "You're safe now."

She opened her eyes.

The vulnerability he saw made it difficult for him to breathe. He wanted to kiss her until all the hurt disappeared and a smile returned to her face.

"I'm…okay," she said, her voice a mere whisper. "When the car stopped, the sounds did, too. I hurt all over. I tried to move, but couldn't. My brothers were on top of me. Cole told me to stay still, to hold on because someone would be coming to help us. I called for my mom and dad and Troy. But no one answered. Cole tried to keep me calm, but his voice faded in and out. When it would come back, he kept telling me someone would be there soon. That someone was a paramedic. By then Cole had stopped talking. Breathing."

Tears gleamed. She wiped her eyes. "Once I recovered and

was out of the hospital, I came to live with my grandparents here in Hood Hamlet. End of story."

Not even close. "And you became a paramedic."

"I wanted to help others the way I'd been helped."

"You are an amazing, brave woman, Leanne Thomas." Christian's admiration and respect grew exponentially. He rubbed her back. "Does the paramedic who helped know you followed in his footsteps?"

"Yes, we've kept in touch." She blinked. "Sorry, I'm usually not like this in front of others."

He brushed the hair off her face. "It's okay."

"Maybe for you." She tried to sound lighthearted and almost succeeded except for her red eyes. "It's my reputation at stake."

"Don't worry," he said. "Your tough-as-nails-never-let-anything-get-to-you reputation is safe with me. I promise I won't say a word."

"Thanks." She peered up at him, looking more shy than tough. "You're only the second person I've ever told exactly what happened during the accident."

"Was Paulson the other?"

"Nick Bishop."

"You were more than friends."

"For like five minutes. We were so young, but figured out really fast we were much better as friends."

"He and Hannah—"

"Were perfect for each other. Two people couldn't have been more different. Hannah's terrified of heights and hates camping and the outdoors. But she made Nick happy in a way no one else could."

"Not even you."

She half laughed. "I wouldn't have wanted to try."

"Thanks for telling me about the accident."

Leanne stared up at Christian. Holding her felt so natural, so right. Her face was so close to his. He wanted to kiss her.

But he couldn't.

She needed a friend tonight, not a lover. Plus, he'd told her he wouldn't bring up kissing again.

Leanne's eyes darkened to that sexy dark chocolate color. They mesmerized him. Her lips parted. She brushed her mouth against his.

Magic. Fireworks. Heaven.

She jerked back. Her cheeks reddened. "I'm so sorry."

"It's okay."

She stood and stared at the carpet. "But I told you no more kisses then I…"

Christian rose. He raised her chin with his fingertips. "No worries. I won't hold it against you."

The corners of her mouth curved upward. That was the response he was hoping for. Christian wanted nothing more than to kiss her again. His gaze wanted to linger on her lips. His tongue wanted to taste her again. But kisses weren't what she needed from him.

Leanne wasn't some random woman he'd met at a bar or the ski resort. She worked with him. She'd rescued him. She deserved more than he was willing to give.

Christian lowered his hand. "What do you say we get this place looking like Christmas?"

CHAPTER TEN

LEANNE stood on a step stool and placed the star on the top of the Christmas tree. The scent of pine filled her nostrils. The multicolored lights blinked. Her vision blurred. She toyed with an ornament. Not because the candy cane needed fixing, but she needed a few minutes to herself.

She couldn't believe she'd told Christian about her family. Nick had pried the information out her during a moment of weakness, but she'd spilled to Christian like a fire hose with its nozzle wide-open. Worse, she couldn't believe she'd kissed him.

Okay, Leanne could believe it. Christian had been here to listen and to hold her. He'd also made her smile and laugh as they decorated the tree and the house. She'd fallen for him. Hard. Just like Alexa had. And Rachel. And probably every other single woman in town. After Christmas, he would start dating again.

Leanne grimaced. What was she going to do? Pretend nothing had changed? Switch shifts?

Paulson and O'Ryan would want to know why. So would the chief. He'd been the paramedic who saved her. She didn't want to disappoint him.

"The tree looks great," Christian said from behind her.

She climbed down and folded up the step stool. "Thanks to you."

"It was a team effort."

If only... Leanne took a deep breath. She forced herself to smile and turned around.

Christian held a stuffed reindeer. "Where does Rudolph go?"

She touched its ear. The reindeer's red nose lit up, filling the dark room with its glowing light. His mouth moved and the song "Rudolph the Red-Nosed Reindeer" played.

"He deserves a special place of honor," Christian said.

She'd received Rudolph during a white-elephant gift exchange. Cocoa wouldn't let Leanne regift him the next year. "I usually stick him in the bathroom."

"Come on, buddy," Christian said to the toy. "Let's put you where you belong."

Leanne placed the lids on the now-empty ornament boxes. Christmas carols continued to play. Flames danced in the fireplace. With all the decorations up, the atmosphere was cozy and romantic.

Christian returned. "It's getting late. I should head home."

Of course he wanted no part of romance. "I'll get your coat."

Christian followed her downstairs. She removed his coat from the closet and watched him shrug the jacket on. "Thanks for helping with the catalogs, listening and decorating."

"That's what friends are for."

Friends. Leanne tried out the word, let it swirl around her mind. Hated it. Maybe once the event was over with she'd look back and laugh at falling for Christian.

She opened the door. Wind howled. A sheet of white fell from the sky.

"The storm moved in early," he said.

A sense of dread filled her. "The roads might be bad."

He took a step toward the door. "I've driven in worse."

"I'm sure you have."

As he moved past her, a knot formed in the pit of her stomach. The thought of him out on the road sent a shiver of foreboding down her spine. "Stay."

Christian stopped. His eyes widened. "You want me to stay?"

Leanne heard the surprise and the confusion in his voice. She was confused herself. He probably could make it home. Still... Not trusting her voice, she nodded.

"Spend the night here," he clarified.

Bad idea. Really bad idea, except... "The visibility and the roads will be horrible. If something happened to you..."

A beat passed. And another. He closed the door. "No sense taking chances. I'll stay."

Relief washed over her. Then she tensed. Oh, no. She'd invited him to spend the night. "I have a guest bedroom."

Leanne said the words so quickly they all ran together.

Christian flashed her a charming smile. "A bed will be better than the couch."

Tension filled the air. Leanne wouldn't mind him sleeping in her bed. Her mouth went dry at the thought.

His gaze met hers. "We should probably call it a night. I have a bag in the truck."

She raised a brow. "That's handy."

"It's for the gym." He sounded slightly annoyed. "I'll be right back."

When he returned, snow clung to his hair. But he looked hot, not cold. The way he stared made Leanne feel like the last chocolate cookie on the plate, and he wanted it. Her. She swallowed. "Need a toothbrush?"

It was his turn to raise a brow. "You have spares for overnight guests?"

"I was at a warehouse store. They only sell packages of six."

"I'd love a toothbrush."

What was going on? This shouldn't be so awkward. She'd slept in the same bunk room with him for over a year. It wasn't as if they were strangers. And this sure wasn't a date. Still nerves threatened to get the best of her. "Help yourself to whatever you need."

"Does that include you if I have a nightmare?" he asked.

"Uh, I..." Leanne needed to get out of here, away from him.

Christian was short-circuiting her brain. She didn't like it. "I'll show you where the bathroom and bedroom are upstairs."

"I'll be right behind you."

And he was. She kept moving to stay ahead of him.

Leanne stood in the hallway, full of uncertainty. She pointed out where Christian could wash and sleep. Now all she needed to do was say good-night. "Thanks again for tonight."

"I'm glad you told me about your family. You're the strongest woman I've ever met." His gaze grew serious. "I'm not talking about how much you can bench press or the number of one-arm pull-ups you can do, either."

Emotion clogged her throat. "Thanks."

Desire filled his eyes. Leanne's heart thundered against her ribs.

The corners of his mouth curved. He tilted his head. His warm breath caressed her cheek.

Leanne wanted him to kiss her. She moistened her lips.

Reality hit her hard and fast like rime ice. No more kissing. "We'd better get to bed. Sleep, I mean. Lots to do tomorrow."

Laughter lit his eyes. "If this nasty weather keeps up, we'll be stuck inside."

That wouldn't be bad. No, she corrected. That would be very bad. She took a step backward and bumped into the hall wall. "Let's hope the storm blows over."

"Do the same rules apply for inside bivvies as ones on ledges?" he asked with a hint of mischief in his voice.

"Rules?"

"What happens on bivy stays there." Christian winked. "Sounds a little like Vegas."

Desire flared. No one would know if anything happened between them. Tempting, yes. But she would know something happened. Leanne had to get away from him before she did or said something she might regret. "Good night, Christian. See you in the morning."

She said the words for as much her benefit as his.

* * *

A phone rang. Christian reached for his nightstand then realized the sound wasn't coming from his cell phone.

He blinked open his eyes. It took his eyes a moment to adjust to the darkness in the room. Not his room. Leanne's guest room.

Wind howled through the trees, but he was warm and comfy in the queen-size bed. The only thing that would make it better was if he weren't alone. Thoughts of Leanne filled his mind, making it difficult to fall back asleep.

What was going on? Christian had spent over a year sleeping in the same bunk room with Leanne. Sure he'd noticed her. Especially during the summer when she wore a tank top and shorts to bed. What guy wouldn't? She had a killer body. Of course, every guy at the station pretended not to notice.

He rolled over, trying to get comfortable.

But he couldn't stop thinking about her. He wanted to know if she was thinking about him. Maybe if he peeked into her room and she was awake

"Christian," a familiar feminine voice called.

Oh, yeah. He wouldn't have to sleep alone, after all. Christian raised himself up on his elbows. He'd hoped to see her standing next to his bed in a sexy nightie or nothing. She was dressed for the storm outside. "What's going on?"

"Sorry to wake you so early," she said. "I received a call-out for a mission. Two teenagers were skiing, but never made it home. Their car is still in the parking lot."

He brushed his hand through his hair. "It sounds nasty out there. You won't be able to do much in this weather."

"They're just kids, Christian. We have to do something."

"I'll come with you."

"There's no room. Hughes is picking a few of us up. He's got a plow on the front of his truck." She smiled softly. "Get some sleep. Make yourself at home. Eat whatever you want."

The thought of her outside in this weather chilled him to the bone. He didn't want her to go, but he couldn't ask her to stay. Not when she had a job to do and people to help. "When will you be home?"

She inhaled deeply. "I have no idea. Just lock the door behind you when you leave."

He wasn't going anywhere. Not until he knew she was back, safe and sound. "I may stick around."

"Whatever you want."

Christian knew exactly what he wanted—her. But that wouldn't take Christmas magic. That would take a Christmas miracle.

Leanne ran outside. She tossed her backpack inside the shell on the back of Hughes's truck and shut the hatch.

Snow swirled around her, pricking her face and sending a chill down her spine. She hoped those two kids found shelter for the night.

She climbed into the pickup truck and slammed the door. Bill Paulson and Jake Porter sat in the back of the dually. "Hey, guys. Where's Moreno?"

"Stomach flu," Hughes said.

Paulson motioned to her driveway. "What's Welton's truck doing here?"

She fastened her seat belt. "It was safer for him to stay the night than drive home in this storm."

Paulson's nostrils flared. "That's the excuse Welton used so he could sleepover?"

"Come on, Paulson." Hughes drove out of the town house development toward the main road. The plow attached to the front of the truck pushed snow out of the way. "I'm sure you've used that one yourself."

"Not with Thomas, I haven't," he said.

"Welton didn't ask to spend the night," she clarified. "I invited him. I do have a spare bedroom."

"So what happened?" Porter asked.

"Not that it's any of your business, but nothing happened." She didn't appreciate his assumption something would. "We're only spending time together because of the Christmas celebration. Thanks to all of you, in case you've forgotten."

"Stop protecting the guy." Paulson's jaw thrust forward. "Knowing Welton, I'm sure he tried something. Pretty much anything in a skirt is fair game with him."

"I don't wear skirts," she reminded. "I told you nothing happened."

Hughes glanced her way with a grin. "You must have shut him down real good when he made his move."

Leanne sighed. "Welton didn't make a move. Why would he when I'm just one of the guys?"

The traction tires sounded against the snow. The wipers continued to sweep back and forth.

"Be careful around him, Leanne," Hughes said finally.

"Real careful," Porter said.

"There's nothing going on." She leaned back against the truck's headrest. "I don't understand why you guys are acting like this."

"We care about you," Porter said.

Hughes nodded. "None of us want to see you get hurt."

Again was left unspoken, but the word hung on the air.

Paulson nodded. "You can do better than someone like Welton."

Leanne knew Christian wasn't the right man for her. He couldn't give her what she wanted—a commitment—and no way could she give him what he wanted—a no-strings relationship. Though that hadn't stopped her from kissing him. Last night and under the mistletoe were the most action she'd had in six months. Okay, her choice. But still…

Christmas wasn't all that far away. New Year's Eve a week after that. She didn't want to be alone. Truth was, right or wrong, she wanted to spend the holidays with Christian. More than she'd wanted anything in a very long time.

Christian couldn't go back to sleep. He understood why Leanne had to go. Helping others, making a difference, was why he'd become a firefighter. But that didn't lessen his concerns about her.

What the hell was wrong with him? All this time he'd worked with Leanne, and seen all the rescues she'd gone out on, he'd never worried about her. He shouldn't be acting and feeling this way over a woman who'd seen more danger on the mountain than he ever had. A woman he wasn't even dating. Or fooling around with. Or kissing.

He showered then headed down to the kitchen where he scrambled a couple of eggs and toasted two slices of wheat bread. Sitting at the breakfast bar in her kitchen, he stared out the window.

Snow continued to fall. Not quite a blizzard, but close. Low visibility. Big, fat, wet snowflakes. Freezing temperatures.

Christian was inside and warm while Leanne was probably out in the middle of it. The thought brought a chill. Yes, she was capable and strong. He didn't doubt her abilities or skill, but anyone was susceptible to hypothermia and frostbite. Even someone as experienced as her.

What little appetite he'd had disappeared. He moved the eggs around his plate with his fork.

Wait a minute. Christian straightened. Rescuer safety was always the priority. Every news station always reported that whenever anything happened on the mountain. OMSAR wouldn't head out in weather like this. Leanne was safe.

Except he couldn't forget the concern in her voice.

They're just kids, Christian. We have to do something.

When kids were involved, emotions ran high and the stakes changed. But Leanne played by the rules. He hoped she was a stickler for them today.

His gaze strayed to the window again. He wished he knew what was going on. Maybe he could find some information…

The radio had no reports. Neither did the Northwest Cable News channel, nor the internet.

Christian released a frustrated sigh. Being on this side of a rescue—the waiting side—sucked big-time.

A blanket of white continued to fall from the sky.

The not knowing grated on his nerves.

This must be how his family had felt when he and Owen had been on the mountain. Maybe even with his firefighting.

Family is so important, Welton. You need to work things out. Compromise.

Christian knew why family meant so much to Leanne now. She didn't have one. But he did. He pulled out his cell phone and pressed the button for his grandparents' house. The voice mail announcement clicked on after the fourth ring.

"You've reached the Weltons," his grandma's pleasant voice said. "We're out and about at the moment. Leave your name and number. We'll call you back when we get home."

Beep.

"It's Christian." Uncertainty coursed through him. This was his family even if he hadn't felt like a part of it for a while. "I wanted to say hi. See what you and Grandpa were up to. It's snowing up here on the mountain. I'm looking forward to seeing you at the Christmas Magic dinner. Talk to you later."

He pressed the end call button on his phone.

Okay, that had taken less than a minute. Leanne would be happy he called. Now what?

Christian needed something to do to distract him from thinking about Leanne out there. He washed his dishes and cleaned the kitchen. He stripped the sheets from his bed and gathered them up with the towel from the bathroom to take to the laundry room.

The door to Leanne's room was ajar.

Christian wondered if she had anything that needed to be washed. He pushed open the door with his foot.

What the…

The flowery, frilly feminine decor of Leanne's bedroom was completely different than the rest of the house. Completely opposite to Leanne herself. Lace, flowers and pink. Not just one shade, but many shades. So…girly.

What was going on? She was one of the guys at the station

and on the mountain. Even in town. Kickass tough and un-emotional. That Leanne wouldn't be caught dead sleeping in a room decorated like this.

Christian remembered how tender and nurturing she was babysitting. The emotional woman he'd held in his arms last night, the one who'd kissed him so gently before thinking better of it. This decor fit that Leanne better.

But he still didn't get it. Her. The woman was a total contradiction. Which one was the real her?

Christian wasn't sure he wanted to know. He liked the softer side of Leanne more than he thought possible. But he didn't want to find himself in a relationship, pushed into a corner having to live up to the demands of someone else. For both their sakes, it would be better to think of her only as Thomas again, one of the guys, a total badass and hardnose, not the attractive, sexy, desirable woman he wanted to kiss again.

And he would. Once she got home from her mission.

Hours later, Leanne arrived home tired, wet and cold. Welton's truck was still parked in her driveway. That surprised her. But pleased her, too.

She pressed the keypad on her garage. The door opened automatically. She dumped her gear inside. A shower and food were her first priorities. She'd unpack and dry things later.

With her boots off, she entered the house.

Christmas carols played on the stereo. The scents of basil and tomato lingered in the air. Oh, man, it smelled so good. Her stomach growled. She climbed the stairs.

Christian stood at the stove stirring something in a pot. Leanne's heart jolted.

He smiled at her. "You're home."

She studied him, feeling much warmer than a minute ago. Home had never felt so good. "The kids found shelter last night. They made their way to Highway 35 once the sun came up."

"Hungry?"

"Starving."

"I raided your fridge and cupboards. Found enough for spaghetti and meatballs."

Her chest tightened. Cocoa used to always make something for her to eat when she returned from a mission. Zoe, too. And now Christian…

"Thanks," Leanne mumbled, not wanting to give in to the emotions swirling through her. "This is exactly what I need."

He poured and handed a cup of coffee to her. "You're wet."

She nodded. Sipped. The hot liquid tasted so good, but she would have preferred a kiss.

"Grab a shower," he said. "After you warm up, we can eat."

A few of his kisses would take the chill right away. But a few of his kisses would never be enough. Leanne wanted so much more. Too bad "more" would never happen with a commitment-phobe like Christian.

CHAPTER ELEVEN

THE next few days passed by in a blur between work at the fire station and in town on Christmas celebration. Ever since the lunch at her town house, something had changed between her and Christian. Something good.

They didn't kiss, but accidental touches and brushes of the hands happened more frequently. Phone calls and texts were exchanged when they weren't together. Which wasn't often. They didn't discuss only the upcoming event, either.

It was…nice.

Leanne was willing to leave it at that. For now. She wanted to ask Christian if he wanted to go on the annual snowshoeing excursion on Christmas Day with her and her friends. All she needed was the opportunity and the nerve.

On Thursday, two days before the big celebration, Leanne went down the mountain to go shopping with her friends at the closest mall.

"I love girls' nights, I mean, days, out." Zoe Hughes stared at the glittery Christmas decorations and lights hanging from the mall's ceiling. She spun around to take in all the sights. The bottom of her skirt flared, showing the tops of her brown leather boots. The woman knew how to take a plain skirt and blouse and turn it into high fashion with a couple of choice accessories. "Especially when it involves shopping with my girlfriends."

"Here, here." Carly Porter wore a purple sweater, faded jeans and a big smile on her face. Life and love with Jake and their nine-month-old baby girl sure agreed with her. "I love being a mom, but I have no time for myself."

Hannah laughed. "You won't until Nicole goes to college."

Zoe smiled at Leanne as if they were partners in crime. "At least we don't have to worry about that."

"I know I don't." But a longing deep inside Leanne ached. She forced a smile. "I doubt it'll be long for you."

Carly raised a finely-arched brow. "You and that hottie firefighter seem pretty close."

Zoe nodded. "He's gorgeous."

"Total eye candy," Hannah said.

Leanne looked at each one of them. "You're married women."

Hannah laughed. "True, but we can still look."

"Looking is all I'm doing myself," Leanne admitted. "I wish we weren't just working on the celebration together."

"Tell Christian that," Zoe encouraged. "He looks like he'd rather be working on you."

Carly laughed.

"The kids love him." Hannah glanced at a group of high school students performing Christmas carols. "They want to know when you two are going to babysit again."

Zoe looked at her. "You and Christian babysat together?"

"We had work to do and thought after the kids went to bed would be a good time," Leanne explained.

"He's totally into you," Carly said.

Leanne was afraid to hope. "You think?"

"Come on," Zoe said. "You know these guys better than anyone. A man doesn't offer to babysit unless he's got ulterior motives."

"Jake did with Carly," Leanne countered.

"Jake was still crazy about Carly even after she'd been gone for six years," Hannah said. "The kids told me you and Christian kissed."

Leanne's cheeks burned.

Zoe tapped her foot. "Spill. Now."

Thinking about Christian's lips against hers made Leanne's temperature rise. "A mistletoe kiss. That's all."

"I remember when Sean first kissed me under the mistletoe." Zoe sighed. "Mistletoe should be mandatory all year long."

"I kissed him."

The three women stared at her. "You?"

"I wanted to get it over with. I was going to give him a peck on the cheek, but he turned his head and I ended up kissing him on the lips."

Zoe pursed her glossed lips. "And?"

"So where did you want to go to look for dresses?" Leanne asked.

Mischief gleamed in Zoe's eyes. "Somewhere where we can find you a dress so sexy the firefighter will be dragging you under the mistletoe all night long."

Heat rose up Leanne's cheeks.

Carly and Hannah laughed.

"You like him," Carly said.

"Of course I like him," Leanne said. "He's a good firefighter."

"Is he a good kisser?" Zoe asked.

Yes. Leanne got chills thinking about his kiss. But she wasn't ready to tell her friends that. She noticed the North Pole Village right in front of them. "Oh, look, it's Santa."

"This is the best mall Santa ever," Carly said. "There isn't a long line. Let's tell him what we want for Christmas."

Leanne would do anything to keep the subject off her and Christian. "I'm game."

"Sure," Zoe said.

"Lead the way, Carly," Hannah said.

Leanne took up the rear. The other women seemed to know exactly what they wanted for Christmas. All she could think about was Christian.

Her turn.

Santa's blue eyes twinkled as she approached his chair. His

cheeks were rosy. He even had dimples. "Do you want to sit on my knee?"

"Uh, no thanks, Santa."

"So what would you like for Christmas?" he asked.

Christian popped into her mind. As if she could ask to find him under her tree on Christmas morning tied with a pretty red ribbon. "I'd like new skins."

The lines on Santa's face deepened. "Skins?"

"For my skis." Leanne thought about skiing with Christian. That had been such a fun day. "I climb and backcountry ski."

"Oh, that would be a practical gift." Santa's blue eyes twinkled behind his gold wire-rimmed glasses. "But I know what you really want."

"You do?" What she really wanted was a family.

Santa nodded. "To get that, you're going to have to believe."

Okay, this Santa was a little weird, but he'd piqued her curiosity. "Believe in what?"

"Christmas magic, Leanne."

"How do you know—" a six-foot-tall elf escorted her away before she could finish "—my name?"

She glanced back, but Santa was already talking to a child dressed in a fancy party dress with matching bows in her hair.

"Ready to shop until we drop?" Zoe said.

The exchange with Santa left Leanne feeling strange, unsettled. Maybe shopping would make her feel a little less off balance. "Sure. Where do you want to start?"

Leanne stepped out of the changing room wearing the perfect dress for the Christmas Magic in Hood Hamlet dinner and silent auction. She wanted to look nice. Christian's family would be there. "What do you think?"

Three pairs of eyes stared at her.

Her heart sunk. "What? Do I look fat?"

"Not at all," Hannah said. "It shows off your figure nicely."

Two little lines formed above Carly's nose. "It's just—"

"You're going to a Christmas party, not a funeral, Leanne," Zoe interrupted.

"Black is versatile," Leanne countered.

"Black is boring." Zoe motioned with her hand. "Turn around."

Leanne did.

"I'll be right back." With that, Zoe disappeared from the dressing room.

Leanne stared at her reflection in the three-part mirror. "A funeral, huh?"

Carly shrugged. "Maybe if it didn't have long sleeves."

"Or a just-below-the-knee hem," Hannah added.

Leanne sighed. "I'm so not good at this."

"No worries." Zoe appeared with a handful of colorful, sparkly dresses. "Because you have me, and I'm great at this."

Leanne gulped.

Zoe held up a yellow dress in front of Leanne. "Washes you out."

Next came a red one with a deep V-neckline. "The color is good. But the design screams nightclub, not community dinner."

Carly and Hannah nodded.

"This purple one might work." Zoe scrunched her nose. "No, too prim and proper. We want Christian's eyes to bug out when he sees you."

"No man's eyes are going to bug out around me," Leanne said, resolved to her fate. "I'm one of the guys. Well, minus the hot-pink toenail polish."

Carly laughed. "You are not one of the guys."

"They only pretend not to notice you," Hannah added.

Leanne made a face. "That's not true."

"All you have to do is crook your little finger and they'd come running," Carly said. "Trust me."

Leanne shook her head. "No way."

"You'll see." Zoe placed a shimmery blue dress in front of

Leanne. Satisfaction filled the former socialite's eyes. "This one."

The little girl inside Leanne, the one who used to live in princess dresses and play with makeup from the time she could open a container of eyeshadow, stared at the dress with a longing so intense she couldn't breathe. But that girly girl had died along with her family. "Isn't it a bit too...sparkly?"

"It's perfect." Zoe shoved the dress into Leanne's hands. "What's your shoe size?"

"Eight."

Leanne stared at the dress. It was so beautiful. Her fingertips itched to feel the fabric, but self-preservation held her back. "If I wear something like this, I'm never going to hear the end of it."

Carly's eyes softened. "You're stronger than most men I know. You can take it."

"But—"

"Put it on." Zoe waved her into the dressing room. She looked at Hannah and Carly. "Keep her in the dress. I'll be back with shoes and accessories. I love makeovers."

"This isn't necessary," Leanne said.

Zoe closed the door. "No, but it sure is fun."

Inside the dressing room, Leanne slipped on the blue dress. The fabric floated over her body, clinging to her hips in a flattering way.

"Do you have the dress on?" Hannah asked.

Leanne glimpsed at her reflection in the mirror. She felt feminine and pretty, the way she'd always dreamed of feeling. But the dress was so not her. She would never be able to pull it off. "Yes."

"Let us see," Carly said.

With a slight hesitation, Leanne opened the dressing room door. Both Carly's and Hannah's mouths gaped.

Leanne stiffened. "I look silly."

"Beautiful." Carly grinned. "You're buying the dress. And whatever accessories Zoe thinks you need to go with it."

"You're not walking out of here without that dress." Hannah said. "Men aren't going to be able to take their eyes off you, Leanne."

She didn't care about men looking at her. Only one man. Christian. She didn't check the price tag, a first for her. "Okay, I'll buy it."

On Saturday, Christian stepped outside the station after shift change. Not a cloud or a snow flurry in sight. Only clear-blue skies overhead for the big event today.

"Perfect weather." He glanced at Leanne, who walked toward her car. "It's got to be Christmas magic."

"You know how fast things can change up here." She tossed a duffel bag into her car. She wore jeans and a red sweater. A candy-cane-striped scarf and Santa hat finished off her outfit. "I hope the weather holds."

Leanne could be so stubborn. He should have known she wouldn't play along even today.

"Ready?" she asked.

Christian was ready to spend another twenty-four hours with her. He'd spent the past twenty-four hours with her. Minus the time driving to calls, responding to calls and sleeping. He didn't want to think about what would happen after today. At least they still had to climb at Smith Rock. "Let's go."

They walked the short distance to Main Street.

"Lots of traffic this morning," Leanne noted.

As they rounded the corner, she gasped. People crowded the sidewalks of Main Street. A group of carolers dressed in Victorian costumes sang. The Hood Hamlet city manager roasted chestnuts on the corner of Main and First. The scent lingered in the cool, mountain air.

"Yes." Christian pumped his fist. "This is awesome."

Lines creased Leanne's forehead. "It's not supposed to start until ten."

"Nobody's going to complain. Come on." He took her gloved

hand in his. The gesture felt so natural to him. "Let's get to the information booth."

Hood Hamlet merchants and business owners smiled. A line of people stood outside the coffee shop. More waited in a line outside the café. The brewpub, serving a special breakfast buffet this morning, also had a wait.

Leanne squeezed Christian's hand. "I can't believe it."

"Believe."

A funny look crossed her face. "You're the second person who's said that to me recently."

"Who was the first?" he asked.

"Santa Claus."

Christian laughed. "Well, Santa knows best."

As they approached the information booth, she slipped her hand out of his hand.

"Here they are," Sean Hughes announced. "The cochairs extraordinaire."

"Hold your applause," Leanne teased. "We have work to do."

Bells jingled.

Christian glanced down Main Street. A beautiful, black horse pulled a red-and-green sleigh decorated with fresh, green garland. Two lanterns, tied with red ribbon, bobbed. The driver looked like something from a Dickens's novel in his stovepipe hat and cap.

Christmas magic. Christian had no doubt. If only Leanne could see it. Feel it. Maybe by the end of the day, she would.

That night, Leanne entered the foyer of the community center where the dinner and silent auction were being held. White lights outlined the doorways. She felt like a fairy princess in her sparkling blue dress, silver shoes and makeup. She wore her hair down at Zoe's urging, something Leanne never did, as well as makeup and jewelry.

The day had been an overwhelming success. The toy drive donation barrels overflowed. Cash registers continued to ring up sales. Not even a traffic jam into town dampened people's enthusiasm. She hoped tonight went as well.

She glided into the multipurpose room, decorated with more white lights, flocked trees, white tulle and shining silver stars. It looked…magical. Compliments of the dinner's sponsor, Welton Winery, and Hood Hamlet Flowers.

"Whoa, Thomas." Her partner, O'Ryan's gaze filled with male appreciation. "You look…nice."

Nice hadn't been the adjective Zoe was after, but Leanne would take it. She'd dressed up for weddings, but never like this. "Um, thanks."

O'Ryan kept staring at her. Okay, her breasts. "You should wear dresses more often."

Everywhere she turned people made similar comments. A few people didn't recognize her. Handsome Johnny Gearhart, the owner of the Hood Hamlet Snowboarding Camp and Academy asked if she had plans for New Year's Eve. The compliments gave her a boost of confidence. Maybe Christian would want to spend the holidays with her.

Leanne saw him on the other side of the room. Christian looked so handsome in his navy suit, dress shirt and tie. She wove her way through the crowd toward him.

When he saw her, his eyes widened. A smile spread across his face. He met her halfway. "You look hot."

Zoe had been right. Leanne shivered with delight. "Thank-you."

"No, thank you." His gaze practically caressed. "So you got plans for New Year's Eve?"

She flashed a flirty smile. "Maybe."

"I'm only half joking," he whispered.

"Me, too."

"Come with me." He led her ten feet to the right. "Oh, look. We're standing under the mistletoe."

"Christian."

"Come on," he urged. "It's tradition."

People stared at them. Apprehension coursed through her.

She didn't like being the center of attention, but she longed to feel Christian's lips against hers again. Even if that meant kissing in public. No one would say anything if it was just a mistletoe kiss. "Make it fast."

As she parted her lips, he lowered his mouth to capture hers.

Sparks. Again. She nearly gasped at the intensity of them. Forget the fireworks a local ski resort shot off on New Year's Eve. Nothing could compare to the pleasurable sensations Christian's kiss brought.

His lips pressed against hers with desire and longing. Matching the pressure, she leaned into him, eager to get closer.

Hot. But no fire extinguisher needed. She wouldn't mind cranking up the heat. She wanted more of his kiss, more of him.

The kiss went on, and on, and on.

Someone cleared his throat. She recognized the sound. The fire chief.

Leanne backed away from Christian, her lips on fire, her cheeks burning and her heart pounding. The kiss left her shaken and wanting more. She took a deep breath to calm herself. It didn't help. "Th-thanks."

Desire shone in his eyes. "We'll take this up where we left off later when not so many people are around."

With her lips tingling, all Leanne wanted to do was kiss Christian again. But that would have to wait until later. She nodded.

He straightened his tie. "We'd better attend to our duties."

During the meal, Leanne didn't have time to eat. She closed two of the silent auction tables and urged people to place bids at the final ones. Not that she was hungry for anything but Christian's kisses.

A giggle welled up inside of her. She felt as if were… floating. Her sling-back heels didn't seem to touch the floor.

She liked feeling special, desired and most especially feminine, a side she'd neglected way too long in order to fit in, a side Christian didn't seem to mind at all.

Maybe he would say yes when she invited him snowshoeing. Maybe she would even have someone to ring in the New Year with.

Leanne touched her lips that still throbbed.

"That was some kiss earlier," Paulson said.

Her cheeks heated. She lowered her hand. A kiss couldn't change everything, but every relationship had to start somewhere. "You know Welton."

"I do." A muscle throbbed at Paulson's jaw. "He's a player, Leanne."

"I've told him what I want." She raised her chin. "He wouldn't have kissed me like that unless he'd changed his mind and wanted that, too."

"You've fallen for him."

"Yeah, I have." No one had ever made her feel the way Christian did. "My heart is still pounding from his kiss."

Paulson grimaced. "Lee—"

"I appreciate the concern, Bill. I really do, but it'll be okay. I know what I'm doing."

He didn't look convinced. "I hope so for your sake."

Her heart brimmed with anticipation at seeing Christian again. This was the perfect time to invite him snowshoeing. "I need to close the final tables. We'll talk later."

Christian stood with his sister and brother-in-law. His grandparents had left with Owen. His cousin had wanted to call it an early night due to his injuries and still using a walker.

"Who were you kissing earlier?" His thirty-eight weeks pregnant sister, Brianna, asked.

"Leanne Thomas." Christian looked for her in the crowd. He couldn't wait to get her under the mistletoe again later. "She's one of the members of the rescue team who found Owen and me."

His brother-in-law, Jeff, gasped. "That's her? We met during the rescue. She cleans up well."

She kissed even better. Christian grinned.

"I thought Kelly turned you off ever getting serious again,"

Brianna said. "Good to know I was wrong. Will Leanne be joining us for Christmas?"

Only people in relationships spent Christmas together. Christian put up his hands. "Whoa, sis. You're way off base. There's nothing serious going on here."

Just the thought made his collar shrink two sizes.

Curiosity filled his big sister's eyes. "But that kiss…"

"Mistletoe and holiday cheer," he explained. "Leanne knows exactly where I stand when it comes to relationships."

Still, Christian hoped Leanne took him up on his New Year's Eve offer. Maybe she'd be willing to settle for something casual, hanging out and having fun. No one would have to know.

Brianna frowned. "You know, just because you don't want to live your life like Dad did, doesn't mean you have to run away from being with anyone."

"I'm not running away from anything."

She looked doubtful. "If you say so, but do you want to end up alone?"

"If I'm alone, it's because I choose to be alone."

"Tying yourself to others, whether it's a woman or your family, won't turn you into Dad. Being with those you care about is a choice. Your choice, Christian."

"That choice still means giving things up." He glanced at his watch. "I'll find you later. I have a couple more things to do."

Christian headed toward the silent auction tables.

"Welton." Paulson cornered him by one of the tall, flocked trees decorated with white lights and red bows. "What the hell are you doing with Leanne?"

Leanne, not Thomas. "If you're talking about that kiss—"

"Everybody is talking about that kiss. Including the chief." Paulson's eyes darkened. "Leave her alone. Leanne deserves better than to have her heart broken by someone who isn't good enough to polish her shoes."

Christian put up his hands as he'd done with his sister. "No hearts are involved, dude. It was just a kiss."

"You might think so." Paulson lowered his voice. "But not Leanne. She's all starry-eyed, and it's because of you. Fix it. Before she's hurt even more."

"Fine. I'll fix it." Christian didn't buy for a minute what Paulson said was true. "But you're overreacting."

Fifteen minutes later, Leanne approached him. She looked radiant and beautiful. Her eyes sparkled, too. But that didn't mean anything.

"Hi." She sounded breathless. "You were right. We've exceeded our toy donation quota!"

"Great." Christian fought the urge to touch her long hair. He liked seeing her finally wear it down. The strands looked silky soft. "Everything's turned out better than I imagined."

"I know." She beamed. "I feel all Christmassy. Speaking of which, I was wondering if you wanted to go snowshoeing on Christmas Day. A group of us go every year."

An invitation for Christmas meant one thing. Leanne wanted a relationship even though Christian told her that wasn't what he wanted. His heart dropped to the toes of his tight dress shoes. Paulson had been right. Brianna, too.

His muscles tensed. Disappointment washed over him.

Leanne Thomas wasn't different. She wanted him to give himself up and live his life a certain way. Be a certain way. Her way.

No way. He'd been honest with her. It wasn't his fault if she chose not to listen. "I'm spending Christmas Day with my family."

"It's only for a couple hours," she explained. "We're never out long so people can get back to their families."

He wasn't about to be pressured into saying yes. Into anything. She'd proven nothing, not even kisses, came without strings. "No, thanks."

"Th-that's okay." Leanne wouldn't meet his eyes. "I saw you with your family. It looks like everything is going well."

"Yeah, the bridge is being mended." He had her to thank for that, but if he said anything she might get the wrong idea.

"I showed my grandfather an empty storefront on Main Street. Told him he should open a tasting room and store up here."

"I'm happy for you, Christian."

Leanne didn't sound happy. She looked a little sad. Not his problem. Better to disappoint her a little now rather than hurt her more later. "Thanks for all your hard work on everything."

Her face brightened. "It was a team effort. Cochairs extraordinaire."

"Yeah, about that." He shifted his weight between his feet. "I only did this to repay you and the rescue team for saving me and Owen. Now you have enough donations for the toy drive and OMSAR has money for gear and training. We're even."

Confusion clouded her eyes. "All this was your way of paying us back?"

Christian nodded.

"We didn't rescue you in order to get something from you."

"You admitted you were happy it happened."

"So did you." Leanne stared into his eyes. "Where did the kisses under the mistletoe fit into this?"

"They were fun." As he said the words he knew that wasn't the whole truth. "You knew I wasn't looking for a girlfriend or anything serious."

No emotion showed on her face. "You made it quite clear."

Rachel waved mistletoe in the air. She motioned him over.

Leanne's lips thinned. "Guess the reporter didn't get the memo about you not wanting a girlfriend for Christmas."

The hurt in Leanne's voice rang clear. He felt like a jerk, but it was better this way. Might as well finish it. "Kissing doesn't make a woman my girlfriend."

Something inside her seemed to turn off. Her eyes dimmed. Christian didn't like it. He touched her arm.

She jerked away as if burned. "Don't."

Her reaction bothered him. "Hey, we're friends."

"No, rookie. We were never friends. A friend doesn't need to pay back another friend for helping them." She spoke with a curt tone that made him feel like slime. "You'd better go see to Rachel. If you blow her off, she'll never go out with you on New Year's Eve."

He opened his mouth to speak, but Leanne was walking away.

Christian's chest felt like it might explode as he watched her go, but what else could he do? Say? They wanted different things in life. She deserved someone who could give her what she wanted. But thinking about Leanne with another guy left a surprisingly bitter taste in his mouth.

"Christian." Rachel saddled up against him in a low-cut sparkly red dress. She held mistletoe over her head. "It's my turn to kiss the firefighter under the mistletoe."

Habit kept Leanne from showing any emotion on her way out of the room. She stopped by the coat check to retrieve her jacket and purse.

Hannah exited the ladies' room and rushed over. "Where are you going?"

"Home."

"The night's still young."

"I'm…" Her voice cracked.

Hannah grabbed her arm. "What's wrong?"

"Nothing. Everything. I feel so stupid." Leanne sniffled. "Christian isn't interested in me. He was only trying to pay OMSAR back for rescuing him and Owen."

"I saw the way he kissed you."

"He's under the mistletoe kissing a news reporter the same way right now." Leanne's throat tightened. "I'm nothing… special."

Her heart shattered. Which made matters a hundred times worse. She had known better.

"Lee—"

"I don't know why I'm so upset. I'm blowing this all out of proportion." She shrugged on her coat. "We aren't involved. We only kissed a couple of times."

"You have feelings for him."

"Had. Past tense." Loneliness allowed her feelings to get carried away. She wouldn't make that mistake again. "Welton's a coworker. Nothing more."

Concern clouded Hannah's eyes. "Want a ride home?"

Leanne had ridden with Zoe and Sean to the dinner, but she could walk home. "Thanks, but I've got it under control."

Hannah hugged her. "Call me if you need anything."

Leanne left without a glance back. After six feet in her high heels on snow-covered sidewalks, she realized walking home wasn't possible. She needed a ride, but the only transportation she saw was the horse-drawn sleigh. She pulled out her wallet and climbed aboard. The driver handed her a wool blanket.

As the sleigh headed down Main Street, the jingling bells irritated her. This ride would be so romantic if she weren't alone. But she was always alone. Probably always would be. Tears welled in her eyes, but she didn't cry.

When she arrived at her town house, half the Christmas lights on her house were out. Just her luck. Inside, petals from the poinsettia plant Christian had given her lay on the floor.

Leanne felt as if she was withering inside, but she didn't know how to make things better. Friends weren't enough anymore. Her job, either. She wanted more. She wanted…

The telephone rang. She ignored it. She didn't check caller ID. Someone was either going to ask why she'd cut out early or tell her how successful the celebration today had been.

If that kind of magic existed, she wouldn't feel so awful and alone.

Christmas magic. She kicked off her high heels. What a joke.

CHAPTER TWELVE

By Tuesday morning, Leanne had resolved not to let Welton get to her. She was a big girl. It was time she acted like one.

She dried the tears from her eyes, put on her uniform and arrived fifteen minutes early for her shift. Not bad considering she hadn't showered on Sunday and Monday.

But she'd realized something important. Welton couldn't give her what she wanted. It was all about being in control with him. Yes, she was hurting, but he could never love her the way she wanted to be loved. He wasn't the kind of man she wanted to be with. Not now. Certainly not long-term or…forever.

The realization didn't ease the ache in her heart, but it helped work through the swirling emotions.

That afternoon, she watched pickup trucks loaded with toy donations leave the station to deliver gifts to local families and other charities.

"You did it, Thomas," Christian said.

Her chest tightened. Time to toughen up. Not be affected by him.

"You were on the committee, too." Then she remembered. He was repaying a debt. The toy drive and Christmas celebration hadn't mattered to him. "Never mind."

An older couple entered the fire station. The man and woman moved slowly as if trying to protect their fragile bones. She carried a round tin in one hand and held the man's hand with her other. They looked familiar. Leanne remembered why. The woman had been a patient.

Grateful for the distraction, she walked over to them. "Hello, I'm Leanne Thomas. How can I help you?"

"I'm Mabel Nichols. This is my husband, Earl. These are for you." The woman's hand trembled as she gave the tin to Leanne. "Snickerdoodles and chocolate chip cookies. I baked them fresh this morning."

Leanne smiled at the couple. "Two of my favorites."

"It's a small way of saying a big thank-you for saving my Mabel's life after her heart attack," Earl said.

"You look well," Leanne said to Mabel. "How are you feeling?"

Mabel's green eyes twinkled. "Much better these days."

Paulson, O'Ryan and Welton greeted the couple. Everyone tasted one of the delicious cookies.

"I remember you," Christian said. "Heart attack. Code save."

A "code save" was someone who wasn't breathing or didn't have a pulse when the rigs arrived, but was alive by the time they arrived at the hospital.

The man kissed his wife's hand with such adoration and tenderness it took Leanne's breath away. She fought the urge to look at Christian. She wouldn't give in to that temptation.

"Today is our sixty-fourth wedding anniversary," Earl said. "We are blessed to have six children, thirteen grandchildren and five great-grandchildren. I'm so grateful to have the love of my life with us this Christmas. She wouldn't be here without all of you."

The love in his voice brought tears to Leanne's eyes. She blinked them away.

After a few more thanks and cookies, the couple left, holding hands like teenagers experiencing the first blush of love.

Hope blossomed in Leanne's heart. Maybe she could find that.

"See," Christian said.

"What?" she asked.

"They wanted to pay us back for saving Mabel's life. The

same way I did with the toy drive and Christmas celebration," Christian explained. "It's no different from me."

Leanne faced him. "There's a big difference, rookie. Mabel said thank you out of gratitude from the very heart that had stopped beating. Earl thanked us from a heart that isn't mourning the loss of his beloved wife this Christmas. But you wouldn't understand that, because you just don't want to feel indebted. Your heart isn't involved because you protect it too much. You're so afraid of being pressured and losing control you can't even let someone do something nice for you. I have only one thing to say to you. Get over yourself, rookie."

With that, she walked away. This was the last shift she had to work with him until after Christmas. Maybe she'd switch a few more shifts so she wouldn't have to see him until the New Year.

Thursday night, customers filled every single table at the brew-bub. The smell of beer and grease wafted in the air. The din of conversations drowned out the Christmas carols playing from overhead speakers. A pine swag decorated with minia-ture lights, holly and pinecones hung around the bar.

Christian sat next to his cousin Kaitlyn. Owen sat opposite them so he had room to rest his broken ankle. A pitcher of beer and a plateful of pretzels sat on the table.

Owen glanced around. "Business is booming."

Christian nodded. "It's been this way since Saturday."

Kaitlyn dipped a piece of pretzel into the brewpub's special mustard sauce. "I've got to hand it to you, Christian. You knew what you were doing with that celebration thing."

Owen nodded. "Imagine what you could do at the winery."

"I had help." Christian took a long swig of Mistletoe Ale, the brewery's special winter ale. The beer tasted good going down his throat. He didn't want to think about Leanne.

"Grandpa said you showed him a storefront," Kaitlyn con-tinued.

Christian stared into his glass. "I did."

Owen leaned forward. "Thinking of moonlighting?"

"My life is here."

Owen's gaze pinned his. "Your family isn't."

Family is so important, Welton. You have no idea how lucky you are to have people who love you so much. Find a way to work things out. Compromise.

Leanne's words echoed in Christian's head. He was trying. "You're all here for Christmas.

"You only work about ten days a month." Owen wasn't being swayed. "That leaves you plenty of time to work at the winery."

Christian took another drink of his beer. "You have it all figured out."

Kaitlyn covered his hand with hers. "We know what Hood Hamlet means to you. But we miss you. Grandma and Grandpa aren't getting any younger."

"We'll have plenty of time to talk about things over Christmas." Christian had lucked out with the shift rotation this year. "I've got Christmas Eve and Christmas Day off."

A familiar laugh floated across the room. The sweet sound wrapped itself around Christian's heart and squeezed tight. Leanne. He glanced across the crowded dining room. She sat with Bill Paulson, Dr. Cullen Gray and Johnny Gearhart.

"Hey," Kaitlyn said. "Isn't that your mountain rescuer? The one you kissed under the mistletoe much to the chagrin of every single man there. Lee-something?"

"The beautiful Leanne." Owen glanced around. "Where?"

"At a table with the three hotties," Kaitlyn said. "Rough life being surrounded by gorgeous men at work and at play."

Owen shifted to get a better view. "The one in the plaid shirt is Bill Paulson. The guy in the black thermal top is Dr. Gray. Not sure about the other one."

Christian stared over his beer. "Johnny Gearhart."

"He's as gorgeous as the other two." Kaitlyn fluffed the ends of her hair. "I'd like an introduction to all three, please. They look totally into Leanne, but there's only one of her. I'm happy to take whoever's left."

Each of Christian's muscles tensed. He rolled his shoulders. *Get over yourself, rookie.*

She didn't know what she was talking about. Not that it mattered. He didn't want a girlfriend. Thomas was free to date whoever she wanted. It was absolutely none of his business what she did or who she spent her nights with.

Owen slid from the booth. He grabbed his crutches. "I'm going over there."

"Sit down," Christian said.

"She saved my life." Owen adjusted the crutches under his arms. "The least I can do is say hello. Coming?"

Christian refilled his glass. "I see her at the station."

That was plenty. More than enough actually.

Outside the Willinghams' log cabin, on December 23, familiar sounding sirens wailed.

Leanne's pulse quickened. She gripped the back of a kitchen chair.

Hannah Willingham placed colorful birthday plates next to the Thomas the Tank Engine cake. "Wish you were with them?"

Leanne pictured Christian in the engine with his helmet strapped under his chin. His eyes would be dark. His lips pressed together in thoughtful contemplation. So serious. So handsome. Such a jerk.

She needed to stop thinking about him.

Leanne released the chair. "And miss my godson's second birthday? No way. I'm so happy Stan traded shifts with me."

Hannah placed two blue candles into the cake. "You'll have to work Christmas Eve and Christmas morning again."

"Stan needs to be with his family." Leanne didn't want to wake up alone on Christmas morning. That was why she always traded shifts over the holidays. The station was the only family she had. She'd rather be there than home. "I'm off in time to go to church and snowshoeing."

"Austin and Kendall can't wait for the snowshoeing."

"They missed Sean and Denali last year."

"Yes, but this year they get Zoe, too."

"Our little group keeps getting bigger."

Hannah wiped her hands on the towel. "Will anyone else be joining in the fun?"

"Not that I know of."

"What about Christian?" Hannah asked.

Leanne stiffened.

"Nothing's going on. I got carried away. Caught up in the holiday spirit and success of the event, that's all."

"And the kiss under the mistletoe?"

"No big deal."

Hannah took a picture of the cake. "You sure about that?"

Leanne thought about the elderly couple at the station. "Positive. I know what I want now."

"What?"

"I want to meet a man, fall in love, get married and have a family."

But that wasn't going to happen until she made some changes in her life. Being one of the guys had served its purpose while she was growing up and finding her way as a paramedic. But she needed to move beyond that if she was ever going to find a man who would love *her,* not who he thought she was.

"That man isn't Welton," she admitted with a pang. "I only wish I knew who he was."

"You'll figure it out," Hannah said. "There are lots of men out there besides those who live in Hood Hamlet. Garrett lived in Portland when we met."

"Jake introduced you to him."

Hannah nodded. "I just had to let myself be open to possibilities."

"I'm open."

Now more than ever. Leanne liked feeling part of a…team wasn't the right word. She was a team at work and at OMSAR. She could only do so much with friends. She wanted to be one half of a couple. Laughing, helping, sharing. With Christian—

Not him, she corrected. Someone else. A man who would enchant her and be enchanted by her, too. One who wasn't afraid to commit his heart, not out of duty or sense of obligation, but out of love.

She sighed. "I wish it would happen soon."

A child squealed from the living room.

Hannah reached for the matches. "It will happen when the time's right. You're just going to have to be patient."

"That's never been a strong point of mine, but I'll try." Leanne stared at the birthday cake, somehow seeing it as three layers with pretty white roses and a bride and groom standing on top. "And hope it's worth the wait."

Christmas Eve arrived with a winter storm warning. Snow fell in the morning and continued into the evening. A few A shift families braved the weather to share a ham dinner at the station with their loved ones. Leanne didn't feel much like celebrating, but being surrounded by so much holiday cheer and joy made it easier to smile.

At ten o'clock that night, right in the middle of a classic Christmas movie, familiar tones sounded. "Rescue 1 and Engine 3 responding to woman in labor, Hamlet Heights, number five."

Leanne jumped into her bunkers and boots. She slid into the medic truck's passenger seat. She glanced at Tucker, her partner for this shift. "Two hours until the twenty-fifth. You think we'll have a Christmas baby?"

Tucker pulled out of the station. Chains had been installed on the rig earlier in the day. "For the kid's sake, I hope he comes before midnight."

"Lots of people are born on Christmas."

He concentrated on the road. Not easy driving with white-out conditions. "I'd bet most of them wished they'd been born another day."

Getting up the hill to the Hamlet Heights development, eight huge custom-built lodges, wasn't easy. The rig made it to the fifth house and stopped in what they hoped was the driveway, in front of two large double doors.

"Want the OB kit or do you want to see what we have first?" Tucker asked.

Leanne would rather transport, but with this weather it was best to be prepared. "Bring it in."

One of the front doors opened. A man walked outside.

Tucker grabbed the kit. "Isn't that Welton?"

Her stomach clenched. He was the last person she wanted to see.

"Glad you guys are here. My sister, Brianna, is in heavy labor. Thirty-nine weeks. She didn't want to spoil Christmas Eve and thought she had more time since she was in labor for seventeen hours with her first. Her water broke and things are moving fast." Christian spoke fast. Nerves. "I thought I was going to have to deliver the baby."

Leanne followed him into the house. Vaulted ceilings gave the modern lodge an airy feel and allowed a twenty-foot Christmas tree to take center stage in the massive living room full of expensive furniture. She'd never seen so many presents in her entire life. "How far apart are the contractions?"

"She wants to push."

So much for transport. Leanne's pulse rate increased. "Where is she?"

"Upstairs."

Leanne entered the large bedroom. She recognized the woman in her early thirties laying on a queen-size bed and the man holding her hand. Both looked stressed and panicked.

"Hi, Brianna. Jeff. I'm Leanne Thomas. We've met before." She wanted to put them at ease. "I'm a paramedic with Hood Hamlet Fire and Rescue. This is my partner, Derek Tucker. Looks like you're getting an early Christmas gift."

Brianna panted. Sweat beaded on her forehead. "I need to push."

Leanne put on gloves. "Let me do a quick exam first, okay?"

Depending on what she saw would determine whether to

go to the hospital or deliver here. Brianna wore a dress so that would make the exam easier.

Christian stood on the other side of Brianna. "You're in good hands, sis."

Brianna moaned.

Leanne saw the top of the baby crowning. Oh, boy. Her muscles tensed. This was something she'd done before, but nothing she did regularly. Her anxiety level rose, but she forced a smile. "Looks like we're going to do this here, okay?"

Brianna nodded.

Tucker got everything out that they needed and prepared the bed for delivery.

"Give us a minute, Brianna." Leanne draped the expectant mother's lower half with sheets and put on the necessary gear herself—gown, new gloves and safety glasses.

Tucker readied the clips, scalpel and bulb syringe. A blanket and hat for the baby were within arms reach. He also had the emergency airway equipment available just in case.

"Okay, Brianna." Leanne ignored everybody else in the room. Nothing else mattered but the mother and baby. "At the next contraction, I want you to push."

Brianna screamed.

"Push."

"Come on, Bri," Jeff said.

The head moved more. So far so good. But until Leanne could see the cord wasn't around the baby's neck, her nerves weren't going to settle down.

Another contraction hit. Brianna pushed. Jeff and Christian encouraged her through it.

The head came out. No cord.

Leanne breathed a sigh of relief. "The shoulders are next."

The delivery went smoothly after that. Before she knew it she held on to a perfect little baby boy. Tears stung her eyes. "It's a boy."

She suctioned the baby's mouth. She stimulated and dried the baby, who wailed at the top of his lungs. A good sign.

The cord was cut and clipped.

She placed the baby on top of Brianna's chest, skin to skin for warmth, and covered him with a blanket. While everyone fussed over the new member of the family, Leanne doubled-checked to make sure Brianna wasn't bleeding excessively. The placenta sill needed to come out.

"We're going to prepare her for transport," Leanne announced.

Christian's eyes gleamed. "Thank you."

She nodded, afraid of sounding too emotional after bringing a new life into the world.

"Yes, thank you." Brianna stared at the baby with love. "I think Thomas sounds like a good name. Don't you, Jeff?"

"A perfect name," he agreed.

Emotion clogged Leanne's throat. She blinked back tears. "Th-thanks."

With help from the engine crew, they made fast work of getting baby and mother to the rig.

Christian followed her out. "Leanne. Wait."

She didn't have time for this. Him. "What?"

"You were amazing."

"It was all Brianna."

"When you get off work tomorrow, spend Christmas with me."

Leanne drew back. "You're spending it with your family."

"I want to spend the day with you, too."

"Yeah, right." She couldn't believe him. "You don't owe me anything for delivering your nephew. It's what I'm paid to do."

"I'm not—"

"I do have to thank you, Welton." She didn't care what he had to say. "Because of you, I figured out I want what that older couple Mabel and Earl have. I thought for a brief second I could have it with you. But we both know I was fooling myself. Wishing for something that wasn't there. The guy I want, the guy who wants to be with me not because he thinks he owes me but because he loves me, that guy is out there. Somewhere. And one of these days I'll find him."

Heart pounding in her chest, she climbed into the back of the rig with Brianna and the baby. Leanne's hands shook as she closed the door. She looked at Christian's sister. "We're going to get you to the hospital as soon as we can."

The rescue rig drove away with its lights flashing. The engine followed without any lights or siren. Christian was cold and covered in snow, but that didn't bother him as much as the way Leanne had spoken.

He wanted to spend time with her, not pay her back. Watching her deliver his nephew had touched Christian's heart. Leanne was so confident, even if he saw a hint of uncertainty in her eyes at the beginning. Brianna had been scared, but Leanne's strength had given his sister courage. And when Thomas arrived…

Tears welled in Christian's eyes. He brushed off the snow, stepped inside and removed his wet shoes. He wanted to share more moments like that with Leanne.

In the entryway, Owen leaned on his crutches. "What's going on with you and Leanne?"

Christian cleared his throat. "Nothing."

"I'm going to ask her out then," Owen said.

"Over my dead body."

Owen raised a brow. "Then why'd you say nothing?"

Christian was the one who'd drawn the line in the sand about no relationship. Leanne was merely reacting to it. "It doesn't matter."

But he couldn't stop thinking about her, wanting to be with her. Maybe he'd been too rash. Maybe he needed to rethink things. No, she'd made it clear tonight.

He'd had his shot at being the guy she wanted, but he'd blown it. She was going to find someone else. "Leanne doesn't want me."

Owen raised a brow. "If you're going to let her go that easily, you don't deserve her."

"Leanne's not the kind of woman you can catch, unless she wants to be caught."

Right now she didn't. Unfortunately Christian only had himself to blame.

The smell of coffee filled the air. Leanne opened her eyes. Half the beds in the bunk room were occupied, the other half empty. Someone snored. And then she realized...

Christmas morning had arrived.

Leanne preferred the buildup to Christmas more than the day itself. She crawled out of bed.

Last night after the baby delivery, they'd only had one other call. A quiet night.

Downstairs, presents filled the stockings hanging on the wall. Everyone on duty got a little something to put in the stockings. This year, she'd put a mini flashlight—a practical gift—and yo-yo—a not so practical one—in each stocking.

Paulson stood with a cup of coffee in his hands. "Merry Christmas, Thomas."

"Same to you." She poured herself a cup of coffee. "Why are you here on your day off?"

"My mom made breakfast for you all."

"That was sweet of her."

He motioned to the window. "It's dumping snow."

Darn. She sipped her coffee. "That'll make for great skiing tomorrow, but not so great snowshoeing today."

"When has a little snow ever stopped us?"

"That was before Kendall, Austin and Wyatt joined the crew," Leanne reminded.

"They're tough kids."

"True, but we still might want to shorten the distance." She hated suggesting that. Snowshoeing with everyone was one of her favorite things about Christmas day. "We have to think about the kids."

Bill thought for a moment. "Yeah, you're probably right."

The tones sounded throughout the station.

"So much for an easy Christmas," he said.

She placed her cup on the counter. "Christmas is never easy." Whether calls came in or not.

Wrapping paper and ribbons covered every inch of the floor of the rented lodge. Christian's nieces and nephews, dressed in brand-new pajamas they'd received last night, tore through presents as if their lives depended on how fast they could open each gift. Even little Emma, with her parents at the hospital with her new brother, shred through presents.

One of the kids handed his grandfather a box. As Grandpa read the tag, Christian fought the urge to hold his breath. "It's from Christian." Slowly his grandfather unwrapped the paper. He lifted the lid off the box and raised the bottle of wine out of the box. Tears glistened in his eyes. "You've been making your own wine."

Christian nodded. "I needed something to do in my time off, Grandpa."

"Besides chasing hot women," Owen said.

Christian ignored his cousin. "The flavor would have been a little deeper if I'd had better barrels."

His grandfather stared at the label. "I'm sure it's fine. We'll try it as soon as we're done here."

"You'll wait until a reasonable hour." His grandmother patted his grandfather's hand. "But I think it's time for Christian's present."

His grandfather carefully placed the bottle back in the box. "I agree."

Emma handed Christian a small box wrapped in holly-covered paper and tied with a red ribbon. "This is for you, Uncle Christian from Grandma and Grandpa."

Based on the size, Christian guessed what might be inside— a key ring or money holder. Possibly a gift card. A practical gift everyone always said. He removed the ribbon.

"Rip it, Uncle Christian," Emma urged.

"Rip it. Rip it," another cheered.

He didn't want to disappoint the kids, so he did as told. The little ones cheered.

"It's a box," Emma shouted.

Christian removed the lid. He opened the white tissue paper. A gold key.

"What is it?" Kaitlyn asked.

"A key." He looked at his grandparents. "What does it open?"

"The future," Grandpa said.

"Whose future?" Christian asked.

"Yours."

The gold key gleamed as bright as a star. His gut clenched.

"I really should say ours. The key is to the empty shop on Main Street you showed me," Grandpa continued. "It'll make a perfect retail and tasting store for Welton Winery. We could even put in a winemaking section. I hadn't realized you were still interested... Since this is your neck of the woods, I thought you might want to be a part of it."

"You're opening a branch of the winery here?"

Grandpa nodded. "I don't think I'm going to be able to take the mountain or the firefighter out of you, so I figured I might as well bring the winery to you."

"What do you want in return?" Christian asked.

"Nothing," Grandpa said. "I butted heads with your father and forced his hand more times than I care to remember. I don't want to do that anymore. I trust you, Christian. Whatever you want to do with the store, we'll work it out. I don't want a grandson who can't bear to talk to me."

Christian stared at the key. Emotion welled up inside him. His grandpa wasn't pressuring him. His family loved him. He wanted to do this. He'd missed being part of the winery. That was why he made wine as a hobby. He'd missed being a part of the family.

"Thanks, Grandpa. It's great." And it was. Christian would be able to do things his way. He was still honoring what his dad told him about not being pressured. But he didn't need to hold everyone at arm's length. Not only his family, but Leanne. "I'll do my best to make you proud."

"You've already made me proud," Grandpa said to Christian's surprise. "I'm sure you'll continue to do so."

He couldn't stop thinking about Leanne. "I will."

As the present opening continued, Owen joined Christian on the couch. "Nice gift."

He looked at the key. "Yeah."

"Maybe you can carry some of my chocolates," Owen said. "Grandpa told me I could make some for the winery."

"Great."

"You don't sound all that excited about any of this."

Christian didn't want to appear ungrateful. "I have a lot on my mind."

"It can't be Brianna and the baby. All reports from the hospital have been good. That leaves…the pretty paramedic."

Leanne was pretty, smart, sexy. "I messed up."

"Apologize."

"She wants a relationship. A commitment. I can't—"

"Better rethink not wanting to make any commitments," Owen said. "You just made a huge one with Grandpa and the wine store."

Christian stared at the key. He had committed to something huge. Yet, it felt good. Right. The same way being with Leanne had felt. He'd worked things out with his family. Maybe he could do the same thing with her. "She still might not want me."

"You'll never know unless you try."

What did Christian have to lose? His pride. His heart. Both, he realized, were worth risking for Leanne. She had told him to get over himself. He had. But he couldn't get over her. She didn't need him, but he needed her. Maybe, just maybe, that would be enough. The least he could do was apologize for being such a jerk to her.

He rose.

So did Owen.

"Where do you think you're going?" Christian asked.

"If she says no to you, she might say yes to me." Owen hobbled on his crutches. "Otherwise we can drown our sorrows together."

Leanne walked out of the Christmas service at church. Singing carols and hearing the message about this special day should have made her feel better. But seeing all the families together, the loving couples and the excited children, only made her feel worse. She trudged through the snow in the parking lot.

A quick dash home to change her clothes then time for snowshoeing. Too bad Leanne didn't feel like going. Unusual for her.

But the kids were counting on all of them being there. She couldn't let them down even if she wanted to spend the rest of her Christmas by herself.

Christmas Day at the fire station was a happy time. Families showed up with presents and joined the crew for meals. Christian didn't see Leanne's car in the parking lot. Maybe she'd caught a ride with someone else. He left Owen in the car and went inside. Two of the B shift wives stood in the kitchen cooking lunch.

"What are you doing here, Welton?" the chief asked.

"Looking for Thomas."

"She left for church a couple of hours ago."

Damn. She might already be somewhere else. "I need to track her down."

"Joining Thomas and Paulson on their annual Christmas snowshoeing trek?" the chief asked.

Leanne had invited Christian to go snowshoeing on Christmas Day. "I can't remember where we're supposed to meet."

"She's probably with Paulson, but Jake Porter, Sean Hughes or Hannah Willingham would know."

"Thanks." Christian headed out the door, ran to his car and slid inside. "She's going snowshoeing."

Owen sighed. "Do you know how many trails there are on this mountain?"

"A lot, but I know who to ask."

Paulson didn't answer his cell phone. Christian drove to Sean and Zoe Hughes's house. No one, not even their Siberian husky, Denali, was home. Next stop was Jake and Carly Porter's house. No one was there, either. Finally he pulled into Hannah and Garrett Willingham's driveway.

Christian stared at the cabin. "I'll be right back."

He exited the car. A single candle burned in the window. Snow angels decorated the front yard, but were being covered by falling snow. He hurried up the snow-covered path and rang the doorbell.

The door opened. Hannah wore the red-and-green apron Leanne had worn when they babysat. "Christian?"

"I need to know where everyone is going snowshoeing today."

She wiped her hands on the apron. "Everyone or Leanne?"

"Please, Hannah," he urged. "I need to talk with her."

"You've already ruined her Christmas."

"I need to apologize. See if she'll give me another chance."

Hannah straightened.

At least he had her attention now. "Please tell me where she is?"

"It'll be easier if I show you." She untied her apron. "Kendall and Austin are there with Jake and Carly. Garrett and I have Tyler and Nicole."

Garrett came to the door. "What's going on?"

Hannah handed him her apron. "I'm going with Christian. I'll be back in a little while."

Garrett looked stunned. "O-kay."

Large snowflakes fell from the sky. Hannah headed to Christian's truck. "We'd better hurry in case they cut their snowshoeing short due to the weather."

She climbed into the truck's backseat, introducing herself to his cousin. "I'm Hannah."

"Owen Welton Slayter."

"She knows where Leanne is," Christian said.

Owen grinned. "I'm glad someone does."

"Take 26 to the snow park," Hannah directed. "The road before the parking lot leads to another small lot and the trail head."

Christian shifted the car into gear. "Thanks, Hannah."

"Don't thank me yet." Concern filled her eyes. "Do you know what you're going to say to Leanne?"

"I thought I'd start with I'm sorry."

"After that?" Hannah asked.

"That I'm lower than pond scum." Christian gripped the steering wheel. "I…I don't know what to say after that."

"You really shouldn't wing this," Owen said.

"Tell Leanne whatever's in your heart of hearts," Hannah suggested.

"This is never going to work," Owen said. "My cousin doesn't have a heart of hearts."

"Well, he'd better find it quick," Hannah said. "And hope a little Christmas magic helps him out."

"You're so screwed," Owen said.

"Thanks, dude." As Christian turned onto the road, he thought about his ex-girlfriend, Kelly. He'd blamed the breakup entirely on her, but he was just as guilty. She'd wanted one thing. He'd wanted another. Neither of them had been willing to compromise. Leanne was different. She didn't want to take. She wanted to give. Even though she'd lost everything, that didn't stop her from giving her all, her heart, to whoever might need it. The crew at the fire station. Their patients. OMSAR. Friends. She wasn't trying to pressure him. She didn't want payment. She wanted nothing in return.

No, Leanne did. She wanted love.

He'd been wrong about her. Oh-so-wrong.

Christian no longer cared about what he wanted. It was all

about her. "I'm going to tell Leanne the truth. And hope it's enough."

"Anything is possible if you believe," Hannah said with sincerity.

He believed, but what about Leanne? Could she believe... in him?

The snowshoeing trip had been a success. Denali, Sean's dog, ran from person to person trying to snag marshmallows. The kids entertained everyone with Christmas carols.

Leanne forced herself to sing along. This was their tradition every December 25. Everyone was here this year. No injuries like last year. She should be having fun.

Leanne stared at her friends. Little Wyatt had fallen asleep in Tim's arms. Rita, Tim's wife, was home cooking, as she did every year because she didn't like the cold. Jake and Carly stood close together, the love for each other apparent with every glance. Zoe leaned against Sean, a picture-perfect couple.

Leanne's heart tightened. She wanted to find that kind of love. But she wasn't like Zoe or Carly or Rita.

Men like Sean, Jake and Tim were hard to find. Not that Leanne would have ever dated any of them when they were single. But love had made the men realize what was really important in life. And what wasn't.

All Christian wanted was to be free. Free of commitment and obligations, to be able to do what he wanted with no pressure. Maybe when he finally fell in love he would realize he didn't have to be so scared of trusting and losing control. It would take a special woman to make that happen. Leanne hoped for his sake, Christian found her someday.

CHAPTER THIRTEEN

Paulson's SUV and Sean Hughes's pickup were parked in the lot. Fresh powder covered the hoods and windshields.

Relief washed over Christian. He pulled into an empty space. "They're still here."

"Do you see Leanne's car?" Owen asked.

Christian didn't see Leanne's red Subaru there. The muscles in his shoulders tensed. "No, but she could have ridden with someone."

He put the truck in Park and set the emergency brake. "Stay inside where it's warm."

Hannah unbuckled her seat belt. "I'm going with you."

"Me, too." Owen opened the door. "Turn off the engine."

Christian didn't think that was a good idea. Owen's face was pale. "You look tired."

"I'm fine."

Christian turned off the engine and exited the truck.

Hannah pointed to a group of people bundled up in hats and coats sitting by a fire. "They're over there."

Christian fought the urge to run. As he walked, snow drenched the hem of his pants. He couldn't wait to see Leanne.

Paulson noticed him first. "What are you doing here, Welton?"

A glance passed between the men. Zoe and Carly shared one, too.

Christian studied each person's face. Leanne wasn't with them. His heart plummeted to his feet.

"Christian!" Kendall and Austin had red, runny noses and pink cheeks. Their eyes sparkled and smiles lit up their faces. "Merry Christmas."

"Merry Christmas to you," Christian said.

Hannah caught up to him. "Merry Christmas everybody."

"Mommy!" the kids shouted.

"I'm looking for Leanne," Christian said.

Another look passed between the snowshoers. Okay, he got it. They were friends of Leanne's. He'd hurt her.

"She left," Kendall announced.

Hannah placed her hand on Christian's shoulder. "Does anyone know where Leanne went?"

Paulson stood. "She had someplace to go, but didn't say where."

"It's a small town." Compassion filled Hannah's voice. "You'll find her."

Christian nodded. He wasn't going to give up now.

"I'm sorry, dude. I don't think I'm going to make it out here much longer," Owen said with a yawn.

"I'll drive you back," Sean Hughes offered.

Tim Moreno held a sleeping child. "I can, too."

"Take Wyatt home for his nap," Sean said. "I've got it covered."

Tim walked to the parking lot with the snowshoes and poles tucked under one arm.

"I'll ride with Carly, Jake and the kids," Hannah said.

Sympathy filled Zoe's eyes. "I hope you find her, Christian." Him, too.

The others walked to their cars. Jake and Sean glared back.

"They don't like me," Christian said.

"You hurt Leanne," Paulson answered.

Regret lay heavy on Christian's heart. "I did."

"You have to understand, we might treat her like one of the guys, but she's more like a sister to us. Always there. Always ready to help out or take off on some adventure to make sure we don't hurt ourselves."

"I didn't mean to hurt her."

"You still did."

"I want to make it up to her."

Paulson didn't say anything.

"I care about her." No, that wasn't right. "I love her."

He eyed Christian warily. "You love Leanne?"

"Yes." There was no doubt. No hesitation. She'd been right. Again. He'd been too scared to admit how he felt, too scared about a lot of things. But no longer. He'd give her his heart, his life if that was what she wanted. "I love her."

"I swear. If you make her cry again, Welton, I'm going to hurt you. Bad."

"Go ahead," Christian said. "I'll deserve it."

Paulson stared at him with respect in his eyes. "You want some company trying to find her?"

"Thanks, but it's Christmas," Christian said. "Go be with your family."

"I should really know where she is today," Paulson said. "But I have no idea. Let me know when you find her."

When, not if. Paulson's confidence bolstered Christian's own. "Sure."

But he had no idea where to start. He thought about what she'd said last night.

I want what that older couple Mabel and Earl have.

They had a long marriage. Kids. Grandkids. Great-grandkids.

Family.

A barrage of images flashed through Christian's mind. The homemade ornaments on the tree. The name LeLe written on the back of the star. The family portrait. The way she reacted whenever someone mentioned Christmas magic.

There isn't such a thing as Christmas magic. If there were, bad things wouldn't happen on Christmas.

Christmas. Not December.

He'd thought she was talking about Nick and Iain, but the two climbers hadn't died on Christmas.

We were on our way home from my grandparents' house. I was playing with a new doll I'd just gotten.

Family. Her family. Christmas Day.

Is your family around here?

Not too far away location wise, but in a completely different place.

The pieces of the puzzle clicked. Christian ran to his car. He knew exactly where she'd gone. It was the one place she shouldn't have to be alone.

He climbed into the truck and turned on the ignition.

Christian didn't want to show up empty-handed. He backed out of his parking spot. The general store might be open. If not, he'd figure something else out.

He turned onto the road. The tires spun on the snow.

Not now. He let up on the gas. He didn't have time to get stuck. If ever some Christmas magic was needed, it was now.

Christian pressed down on the accelerator. The car jerked forward onto the highway.

All he had to do was get to Leanne. He loved her. Even if she didn't need him or want him, maybe she'd still let him spend Christmas with her. Because he really didn't want to spend today without her. He didn't want to spend another day without her.

He only hoped he could convince her to give him another chance.

"Merry Christmas." Leanne placed an evergreen wreath with pinecones, holly and a weatherproof red bow in front her family's headstone. She looked at each name with a pang in her heart.

"I love you." Tears stung her eyes, but she didn't blink them away. She touched the headstone with her gloved hand. "I miss you."

But it wasn't the same heart-wrenching emotion the first few Christmases had brought with them. When she was younger, she used to come here all the time. To think. To talk. But she didn't need to do that now. She came only once a year. On the anniversary of the accident. The one day—okay, a few hours—she allowed herself to be…herself. A few hours weren't enough anymore.

"I wonder if you'd be surprised by the person I've become. I'm not sure I can keep it up much longer. I need…more. A family like we had."

She had friends. Good friends, but she wasn't with them today except for snowshoeing. She wanted to be celebrating the holiday with family, not standing in a cemetery alone.

"I hope it's not too late."

A gust of wind came out of nowhere. Snow blew from tree branches. It sounded almost like a whisper.

LeLe.

She froze. The hair on the back of her neck stood up. Only her family and Nick had ever called her that. All of them were buried in this cemetery.

She glanced around. No one was there.

Relief washed over her. For a second she thought she might see the Spirit of Christmases Past. Okay, now she was being really silly. She laughed.

Maybe it was a sign she wasn't supposed to ignore her LeLe side anymore. And she wouldn't. No matter what people thought.

"LeLe."

The sound of her name was clearer this time and hung on the air. She turned.

Christian strode through the snow with a box full of poinsettia plants in his gloved hands. A puff of condensation accentuated each breath. He wore a green jacket, khaki slacks, boots and a wool beanie on his head.

Gorgeous. Not that she wanted him. Still, regret clawed at her heart.

He stopped in front of her.

She raised her chin. "How did you know I was here?"

"Christmas magic."

"Yeah, right, so—"

"Let's put these down first. Then we'll talk."

Christian placed two poinsettia plants on each side of the wreath. Red foil covered the plant pots, the effect very pretty and Christmassy.

Four plants remained in the box. She stared, confused. "Who are those for?"

"Your grandparents, Nick Bishop and Iain Garfield."

Her mouth gaped. "How…"

"Show me where they are."

She led him to her grandparents' grave. She'd already placed a wreath there. "They were in their seventies when I came to live with them. They died within two weeks of each other, right after I turned eighteen. I think they tried to hang on until I was old enough to be on my own."

"Eighteen is still young."

She was about to shrug. She was so used to acting tough and appearing as if nothing bothered her. The truth was she had been young. Too young to be on her own. "Yeah. I still hadn't graduated high school."

"They would be proud of the woman you've become."

"I hope so." Her grandparents had done the best they could. But they hadn't been prepared to raise another child at their age. She'd had few rules except to make good grades and be home by bedtime. She could have gotten into a lot more trouble if she'd fallen in with a different crowd. "I tried to stay out of their way and be good. It mostly worked."

"Mostly?"

"Except when I went against my better judgment and took off with the guys."

"They became your family."

Her first instinct was to say yes. Jake and Nick were the ones who attended her high school graduation, but they probably would have come anyway since Bill was graduating, too.

"The closest I've had in a very long time." But she wanted more. "They say I'm one of the guys, but I'm not always treated that way. Whenever something big went down, like when Nick was missing or Sean wanted to get Zoe back, I was the one left to stay with the wives, girlfriends and kids. Even though I tried hard to be one of the guys, when push came to shove I'm still a girl."

"I'm glad you're a girl."

She straightened. "Me, too."

"So who are you planning to spend Christmas with today?" Christian asked.

"No one," she admitted.

"You prefer being alone."

"No."

"Why aren't you spending Christmas with anyone?"

"I'm spending it alone."

"No one invited you."

"You did last night." She took a deep breath. "I could have asked—"

"Not your style."

No, it wasn't. She couldn't believe he knew her so well. "It's okay. Nick used to always invite me over, so it's not like I've been alone since my grandparents died."

"Only since Nick died. Eight years."

"Cocoa was here for three of those Christmases."

Accusation filled Christian's eyes. "That doesn't make it right."

"It's no one's fault. Things changed when Nick died," Leanne explained. "People had their own grief and pain to deal with. Carly and her parents moved away. Jake was so busy helping Hannah and the kids. Tim had just met his future wife and was head over heels in love. Bill was…well, Bill."

Christian started to speak then stopped himself. He handed her one of the poinsettia plants. "This is for Nick."

She walked to his gravestone. She placed the plant on the ground. "Nick loved Christmas. He wore a Santa hat the entire month of December. Even when we were in high school. He was a lot like my oldest brother, Cole."

"Which is why he called you LeLe."

She nodded. "He was a good guy. He knew exactly when I needed a friend or a big brother. Or when he needed to push me out of my comfort level to try something new."

Christian held the remaining plant in his hand. "Where's Iain?"

"His parents didn't want him buried here on the mountain."

Christian placed the poinsettia next to Nick's. "They're probably together."

The gesture touched her. She shoved her gloved hands in her pockets. "Thanks for bringing these by. But I'm not really sure why you did or why you're even here. You don't owe me anything."

"I know, but I wanted to see you."

Her pulse quickened. "On Christmas?"

He nodded. "I went by the station, but you'd already left. I ended up at the snowshoe trailhead."

"No one knew where I was going."

"I know," he said. "I was feeling pretty lost and a little desperate."

"Desperate?"

"Yes, until I figured out where you would be." He motioned to the poinsettias. "I didn't want to show up empty-handed so I stopped by the General Store."

"It's not open on Christmas Day."

"I called Mr. Freeman."

She didn't get it. "You went to a lot of trouble."

"You're worth it," he said. "As you said, it was time to get over myself."

The air rushed from her lungs. Her mouth gaped. That was what she'd said to him at the station.

He took her gloved hand in his. "Come with me."

A million questions filled her mind, but she kept quiet.

Christian led her to a trail at the far side of the cemetery. Her boots crunched on the snow as they headed up. Tall trees flanked the path. She had no idea where they were going. She also knew they weren't prepared for a hike in this kind of weather without any gear or water.

But she kept her mouth shut.

He stopped in a clearing, surrounded by snow-covered pine trees. A perfect Winter Wonderland setting. Snow flurries fell down on them as if they were standing in the middle of a snow globe.

Christian took a deep breath. "I'm sorry I've been such a jerk."

Her heart stuttered. He wanted to apologize. That was why they were here and he'd brought the flowers. Disappointment shot through her.

"Apology accepted." She looked at a snow-laden branch, then at an intricate snowflake spinning and twirling its way to the ground. She would stare at anything if it meant not having to meet his gaze again. "Thanks for bringing the poinsettias, too. We're more than even now."

"I'm not trying to repay you, Leanne. You have to understand. In my life, strings were attached to everything. There was always pressure to do what others wanted. Because of that I wanted everything to be my choice, be under my control." He took her hand. "You made me see I went too far. Caring for someone is not an obligation or pressure. It's mutual giving. Can you forgive me?"

Her throat tightened. She blinked back the tears in her eyes.

"I forgive you," she said. "I'm sorry for being so emotional. I've kept that side hidden for so long, when it comes out it's hard to control."

"Please don't feel the need to control it around me. You're the most capable, self-reliant woman I've ever met. You don't need anyone. I thought I didn't need anyone, either. I tried to be entirely independent, but that isn't the best way to live. It's not what I want anymore. I need you. I want to be part of your life."

"As a friend."

"More than a friend."

"Oh, you want someone to kiss on New Year's Eve."

"You know me well," he admitted, to her regret. "But I don't just want to kiss anyone. I want to kiss you."

Her heart wouldn't survive. Even if her lips wanted to kiss him again.

"I also want to kiss you on Valentine's Day, St. Patrick's Day, Easter, Fourth of July, Halloween, Thanksgiving and Christmas," Christian continued. "For the next, say…sixty-four years. I love you, LeLe."

Her heart skipped a beat. Maybe three. "You love me?"

He nodded. "I think I may have fallen in love with you the minute you appeared in the snow cave. I'd never been happier to see someone. Granted, I was slightly hypothermic at the time. But I should have known it the second I kissed you under the mistletoe in the kitchen."

She listened in disbelief. "I…"

"I may be younger than you and an idiot at times, but I learn from my mistakes. If there's one person in this world who I can trust, it's you. I'll never have that with anyone else because no one else gives so much of herself for so little in return." The sincerity in his words rang true. "I don't want to lose you. I don't care what anyone says or thinks, not even the chief. If you want me, just say the word. I'm yours."

She struggled to breathe. Her heart raced, matching her pulse rate. This was more than she imagined, more than she'd ever dreamed.

"Word." Leanne rose on her tiptoes and kissed him hard on the lips. No one was watching. She didn't have to hold back. She poured all her emotion, all her heart into the kiss. Nothing had ever felt so right. "I want you. I need you. I love you."

"I love a woman who knows what she wants and isn't afraid to say it." He grinned. "Marry me."

Leanne sucked in a cold breath. She opened her mouth to speak, but nothing came out. He had to be joking, right? She was afraid to ask.

"Oops. Forgot something." Christian took her hand and

kneeled in the snow. From his pocket he pulled out a plastic container, the kind found in a gumball machine. Inside was a toy ring. "Will you marry me, LeLe?"

This couldn't be happening. At any moment she would wake up at the station. Except she felt the snow hitting her face and the cold air as she inhaled. "You're serious."

"Very." He showed her the plastic ring. "I hope this will do until after Christmas. No jewelry stores are open today. It was either this or a mood ring."

Her mind reeled. "But you didn't want a girlfriend for Christmas."

"No, but a fiancée for New Year's sounds perfect."

Her heart slammed against her chest. He was serious.

"If I don't rope you into marrying me, you might take off up the mountain, and I'll never catch you. Just like when we went backcountry skiing. We've both shut ourselves off, Leanne, and now we need to take the same sort of risk we take every day on the job, and trust each other, not waste more time. Let's not be afraid to live the life we both want."

His gaze captured hers. She couldn't have looked away if she wanted to. The love in his eyes sent a burst of tingles shooting through her. Joy overflowed. "Oh, Christian…"

"I'm a firefighter. I'm trained to put out fires." He touched his chest, right where his heart would be. "The one right here. You ignited. I want it to keep burning. What do you say, LeLe? Marry me?"

She'd never imagined feeling so cherished before. This was the fairy tale. At least as close as one got these days. Leanne grinned. "Using my name doesn't always guarantee a yes."

Hoped gleamed in his eyes. "But I'm sure it can't hurt."

"You realize I'm not just one of the guys."

"You like pink, frilly things. Flowers and lace, too."

"How did you know?"

"I saw your bedroom, though it confused me."

"I'm sure it did." She laughed. "I used to be a little princess-type girl. But after my family died and I came to live in Hood

Hamlet, I needed to fit in somewhere. Anywhere. I missed my brothers so much. When I met Bill and Jake and Nick, they reminded me of Cole and Troy so much. I wanted to be friends with them so I did everything I could to be one of the guys. It carried on to the station."

"I get it." Christian caressed her cheek with the side if his fingertips. "But all that matters now is you're my girl. Whether you're kicking my butt skiing or dressed from head-to-toe in pink sparkly stuff or in your bunkers."

"I am your girl. I think somehow I always knew even when I tried to talk myself out of it." Full of love, contentment flowed through her veins. "My answer is yes, Christian. I'll marry you."

He kissed her on the lips. "Merry Christmas, LeLe."

She stared at the snow falling and clinging to his hair. So handsome. So strong. And hers.

"Merry Christmas, Christian." She placed her palm on his chest and felt the beating of his heart. "Maybe there is a little Christmas magic in Hood Hamlet, after all."

* * * * *